"It's hard to get really excited about the race knowing Bruce is going to win anyway," Lois said.

"Maybe not," Elizabeth said. "Lois, do you have your pledge card with you?"

"Sure," she said, pulling it out of her book bag.

After a few moments of calculating, Elizabeth turned to Lois with a smile. "Most of your pledges are for small amounts, but you have a ton of them," she said.

"Added all together, they come to eighteen-fifty per mile! With a few more pledges, I could catch up to Bruce." Lois was ecstatic.

"But even if you get as much money as Bruce, you'd still have to ride the whole way to win," said Elizabeth. "Do you think you can make it?"

A look of determination crossed Lois's face. "Don't worry, Elizabeth. I'm going to ride as hard and as long as I possibly can. Maybe I won't go the whole thirty miles, but by the time I'm done, Bruce Patman will think twice about bugging me again!"

SWEET VALLEY TWINS

Lois
Strikes
Back

Written by
Jamie Suzanne

Created by
FRANCINE PASCAL

A BANTAM SKYLARK BOOK®
NEW YORK • TORONTO • LONDON • SYDNEY • AUCKLAND

RL 4, 008-012

LOIS STRIKES BACK
A Bantam Skylark Book / April 1990

*Sweet Valley High® and Sweet Valley Twins are trademarks of
Francine Pascal*

Conceived by Francine Pascal

*Produced by Daniel Weiss Associates, Inc.
33 West 17th Street
New York, NY 10011*

Cover art by James Mathewuse

*Skylark Books is a registered trademark of Bantam Books, a division of
Bantam Doubleday Dell Publishing Group, Inc.*

ISBN 0-553-15789-2

Published simultaneously in the United States and Canada

Bantam Books are published by Bantam Books, a division of Bantam
Doubleday Dell Publishing Group, Inc. Its trademark, consisting of
the words "Bantam Books" and the portrayal of a rooster, is Registered
in U.S. Patent and Trademark Office and in other countries. Marca
Registrada. Bantam Books, 666 Fifth Avenue, New York, New York 10103.

PRINTED IN THE UNITED STATES OF AMERICA

OPM   0 9 8 7 6 5 4 3 2 1

Lois
Strikes
Back

One

◇

"Jessica, I think we have about thirty seconds to get to homeroom," Elizabeth Wakefield told her twin sister. "Do you think we could at least head in that direction?"

"Just a minute," Jessica replied. "I want to ask Tamara if she's going to the Unicorn meeting at lunch."

"Didn't Mr. Davis tell you he'd give you a detention if you were late again?" Elizabeth asked patiently.

Jessica stood on her tiptoes and searched the corridor of Sweet Valley Middle School for her friend. "Oh, well," she said casually. "I don't see Tamara anywhere. Let's go."

"You know, Lizzie," she added as they walked down the crowded hallway, "you really shouldn't worry so much."

Elizabeth sighed. On the outside, the Wakefield twins were identical. They both had shoulderlength blond hair and blue-green eyes. They even had twin dimples in their left cheeks when they smiled. But on the inside, they couldn't have been more different. Elizabeth was the quiet, more serious twin. She liked reading, horseback riding, and working on *The Sweet Valley Sixers*, the sixthgrade newspaper she had helped found. And though she enjoyed having fun as much as anyone else, she didn't mind helping out when there was work to be done.

Jessica was too busy thinking about boys, fashion, and the cheerleading squad to worry much about anything else—schoolwork and chores included. She was a member of the exclusive Unicorn Club, which only the prettiest and most popular girls were asked to join. Elizabeth felt that most of the Unicorns were snobs, and so she chose her own set of friends, almost none of whom were Unicorns. But as far as the Unicorns were concerned, they were as good as royalty, and so they chose purple as their club color. Every day, they would wear something purple.

In spite of all of the twins' differences, they had a special bond that only twins could share.

When they got to homeroom, Jessica slid into a seat next to her friend, Lila Fowler. Elizabeth walked to the front of the room, where she sat across from *her* friend, Amy Sutton.

"What's that?" Elizabeth asked Amy, pointing to a photograph of a shiny mountain bike that was propped up on Mr. Davis's desk.

Amy pushed a strand of her straight blond hair behind her ear and shrugged. "I don't know. Winston Egbert asked Mr. Davis about it, and he just said he'd tell us when everyone got here."

The second bell rang, and the class began to quiet down. Mr. Davis took attendance. Then he looked up and said, "Good morning, everyone." Smiling, he added, "I have some interesting news for you today."

Everyone looked at one another. Mr. Davis seemed very enthusiastic about his news, whatever it was.

"I suppose most of you know that the PTA recently raised money to buy new books for the library. Well, the effort was so successful that the PTA has another project in which they would like us to participate."

Elizabeth had been excited when the new books for the library had arrived. The librarian, Ms. Luster, had purchased several Amanda Howard mysteries. They were Elizabeth's favorites.

"The PTA has decided," Mr. Davis continued, "it would be a good idea for the library to have several video tape recorders and a selection of tapes."

"Can we get the *Indiana Jones* movies?" someone called from the back of the room.

"What about *Batman*?" someone else asked.

Mr. Davis smiled. "I'm afraid instructional tapes are what the library had in mind."

Amy raised her hand. "What kind of a fund raiser is it?" she asked.

"A bike-a-thon," Mr. Davis answered.

"How does it work?" Winston called out.

Mr. Davis glanced at a sheet of paper he was holding. "Each participant will get as many sponsors as he or she can. Each sponsor agrees to pay a certain amount for every mile the participant rides."

Lois Waller raised her hand. She was a shy girl

who was self-conscious about her weight. She usually didn't say much in class because she was afraid someone would make fun of her.

"Yes, Lois?" Mr. Davis said.

"Can the sponsors put up any amount of money?"

"Yes. It can be as little as a penny a mile." Mr. Davis chuckled. "Of course, larger amounts are welcome, too."

"Is there a prize?" Jessica called from her seat.

"There certainly is." Mr. Davis picked up a photograph of a mountain bike. "This is the latest thing in bicycles, I understand." He handed the picture to Elizabeth. "Pass this around, please," he said.

Elizabeth was impressed. She had a bike, but it wasn't nearly as nice as the one in the picture. This one was bright blue with wide tires and a leather seat. It had eighteen speeds! After carefully studying the photograph, she handed it to Patrick Morris, who was sitting behind her. He took it eagerly. Mr. Davis began to explain the rules of the contest.

"The winner will not necessarily be the person who finishes first," he said. "The winner will be the student who makes the most money. That means getting a large number of pledges and then completing as much of the thirty-mile course as possible."

"*Thirty* miles?" Winston called out. "Isn't that a lot?"

"Yes, it *is* a long ride," Mr. Davis agreed, "but I'm sure a lot of you can do it." He looked down at his information sheet again. "The PTA will give a special prize to every student who crosses the finish line."

"When can we start getting our sponsors?" Amy asked.

Mr. Davis picked up a stack of cards from his desk. "These are your sponsor cards; I'll pass them out right now. The bike-a-thon will take place one week from Saturday. And remember, pledges that aren't collected don't count toward your total."

He began handing out the cards. When Elizabeth got hers, she quickly looked over the card. There were lines for each sponsor's name, address, and amount of the pledge. In her head, Elizabeth began making a list of people she would ask to sponsor her. She couldn't wait to begin.

"I can't believe the PTA picked such a terrific

prize," Amy was saying as she and Elizabeth walked down the hall to their first class. "I would love to win that bike."

Elizabeth felt a tap on her shoulder and turned around to find Jessica standing behind her. She had an odd look on her face.

"Jess, is something wrong?" Elizabeth asked. "You look upset."

Jessica sighed dramatically. "It's the bike-a-thon," she said sadly. "I really want to win that bike. Especially since mine is falling apart."

"I'd like to win it, too," Elizabeth said. "We got our bikes at the same time, remember?"

"Well, that's why I'm upset," Jessica said. "It's going to be nearly impossible for me to get sponsors. Everyone else can get pledges from both their parents and all their brothers and sisters, but *I'll* have to divide our family up with you."

Elizabeth had an uncomfortable feeling. Was Jessica suggesting she drop out of the contest? "I'm sure Mom and Dad will sponsor us both," she told her.

"They might, but no one else will," Jessica said. "Steven won't."

"I'm not sure he'll sponsor either one of us,"

Elizabeth said. "You know how Steven can be about money."

The twins' fourteen-year-old brother, Steven, was known for his stinginess. Of course, he was *better* known for his huge appetite.

"So what are we going to do about it?" Jessica demanded.

"We'll figure something out, Jess," Elizabeth said. "I'm sure of it."

"I think Jessica wanted you to quit," Amy said with a giggle as soon as Jessica was gone.

"I know," Elizabeth replied. "But don't worry. I don't give in that easily!"

"All anyone can talk about is that bike," Julie Porter said at lunch.

"I think we should run a feature on the bike-a-thon in the *Sixers*," Elizabeth said. "We could print the details of the contest, and maybe even a map of the route."

"Maybe we could do a special issue on the contest," Amy suggested.

"Can I sit with you guys?"

Elizabeth looked up to see Lois Waller standing over them, a very full tray in her hands. "Sure," Elizabeth said. "Sit down."

"I heard you talking about the bike-a-thon," Lois said as she settled into a chair. "I'm really excited about it!"

Elizabeth and Amy exchanged glances. Lois was so self-conscious about being overweight that she hardly ever participated in any activities. Trying to hide her surprise, Elizabeth asked, "Are you going to ride?"

"Definitely!" Lois replied.

Now Elizabeth was really surprised.

"You want to win the bike?" Amy asked.

"Yes! I have an old bike—I'll have to ride that one in the race, I guess—but I'd love to have that mountain bike."

"How come?" Elizabeth asked.

"I'm trying to get a paper route," Lois said proudly. "And a new bike would make it much easier."

"A paper route?" Amy asked. "How come I never thought of that? Tell me all about it!"

"That bike can go anywhere!" Patrick Morris said.

"It can go up mountains, down dirt trails, even over sand," Ken Matthews added.

Winston Egbert swallowed a huge bite of his

grilled cheese sandwich. "My parents said they would get me a bike like that for my birthday, but if I won it, then maybe they'd get me a chemistry set."

"When I was at the bike store in the mall last week," Ken said, "I saw this bike that had—"

"Matthews!" Bruce Patman interrupted as he came up to the table. "Don't forget about the soccer game after school. We've decided to let a few of you puny sixth-graders play with us." Bruce was a seventh-grader.

Ken smiled at Bruce. Ken was small for his age, but he was a good athlete. "Better watch out. If I'm not on your team, Patman, you're going to lose!"

"Yeah, I'm really scared," Bruce said with a smirk. His family was one of the richest in town, and Bruce thought that gave him the right to say anything he wanted. Most people at school thought he was a snob, but all the Unicorns thought he was the cutest boy in the entire seventh grade.

"Hey, Bruce," Patrick said, "did you hear about the bike-a-thon?"

"Sure," Bruce replied, "everyone is talking about it."

"Are you going to enter?" Ken asked.

Bruce shrugged. "I don't know. I have an OK bike already, remember?" Bruce had a silver Italian racing bike. His parents had sent it to him when they were traveling in Europe. It was more than OK; it was one of the coolest bikes anyone at Sweet Valley Middle School had ever seen.

"If I did enter," Bruce continued, "there's no way the rest of you guys would have a chance. I could easily ride thirty miles on my racer."

"Then stay out of it," Winston muttered.

"Even if I do, there's no way you could win, Egbert. I've seen that broken down thing you call a bicycle."

Winston's ears turned bright red, the way they always did when he was embarrassed, but he didn't say anything.

Bruce turned to Ken. "Don't forget, Matthews. Meet us after school at the field."

"I'll be there," Ken managed to choke out over a bite of his peanut butter sandwich.

Bruce was about to walk away when he caught sight of Elizabeth, Amy, Julie, and Lois at the next table. He walked over to where the girls were sitting and looked down at Lois's tray.

"What do you want, Bruce?" Elizabeth asked

coolly. Bruce Patman was one of her least favorite people.

"That's not very nice, Elizabeth. I just came over to say hi."

"Well, hi." *And goodbye*, she thought.

"Lois, that's quite a lunch!" Bruce said.

Lois didn't say anything, but she put her forkful of spaghetti back down on her plate.

"Let's see what Lois Waller has for lunch today, everybody," Bruce said in a loud voice.

Everyone at the surrounding tables fell silent.

"One huge helping of spaghetti, two pieces of garlic bread, chocolate milk—" Bruce called out.

"Bruce, be quiet," Elizabeth hissed. But Bruce just ignored her. "What's this? A piece of cake, *and* ice cream? Lois, I don't think you need both of those, do you?"

Lois didn't answer, but Elizabeth could see her eyes starting to tear up.

"We're going to have to change your name to Lois Walrus if you keep going at this rate," Bruce said loudly. Laughter broke out at several of the surrounding tables.

Bruce waited a few seconds for Lois to react. When she didn't, he finally said, "Well, enjoy your banquet, Lois." Then he strolled back to his friends.

"Don't let him upset you, Lois," Amy said as soon as Bruce was gone.

"Amy's right," Elizabeth said. "Everybody knows what a jerk Bruce Patman is."

"If you just ignore him, he'll eventually leave you alone," Amy added.

"For a while," Lois said. "Then he always starts in on me again."

Elizabeth didn't know what to say. Lois was right. She was always being teased by Bruce, and it didn't seem likely that he was going to give up on her.

"I don't know what to do," Lois said. She pushed her tray away. "More than anything, I wish Bruce Patman would leave me alone!"

Two

◆

"So what are we going to do, Mom?" Jessica
asked.

Mrs. Wakefield sat at the kitchen table, surrounded by wallpaper and carpet samples. She
worked part time as an interior designer, and
when she was very busy at the office, she sometimes had to bring work home.

"Mom?" Jessica repeated.

Mrs. Wakefield finally looked over at her daughter. "I'm sorry, Jessica. What are we going to do
about what?" she asked.

"The bike-a-thon," Jessica said with a sigh.

Before Mrs. Wakefield could answer, Mr. Wakefield and Steven came into the kitchen, each carrying a large paper bag.

Steven and Mr. Wakefield both had wavy brown hair and brown eyes. Even though they would never admit it to him, the twins thought Steven was beginning to look a lot like their father, a very good-looking man. Some of their friends even thought Steven was cute!

"What do you have there?" Mrs. Wakefield asked.

Jessica had already guessed from the delicious smell coming from the bags. "Chinese food," she said happily.

"That's right," Mr. Wakefield said. "After I picked Steven up at basketball practice, I decided to go over to Wong's."

"It looks like you bought everything on the menu," Mrs. Wakefield commented.

"Steven helped me decide," Mr. Wakefield said.

Jessica laughed. "No wonder there's so much food!"

Just then Elizabeth, who had been upstairs doing her homework, walked into the kitchen. "What's so funny?" she asked.

"My loving sister is making fun of my appetite,

for a change," Steven said with a grin. "I can't help it if I'm a growing boy."

"You're going to be growing out instead of up if you keep eating the way you do," Jessica warned.

Steven patted his flat stomach. "I've still got plenty of room in here."

"Why don't we eat while the food's still hot," Mrs. Wakefield said. "Steven, please help me move these samples into the living room, and girls, you can help your father set the table."

Jessica inched her way toward the door. "I'll be right back—" she started to say.

Mrs. Wakefield cut her off. "Jessica, it will go faster if you both help."

Jessica made a face, but she knew when she was trapped.

A short time later, the family was sitting around the table, surrounded by cartons of egg rolls, fried rice, and other Chinese specialties. As soon as they had sat down, Jessica once again told everyone about the bike-a-thon, and explained the twins' problem.

"So," she finished, "we'll probably have half the sponsors everyone else does, because we've got to split everyone in two."

"Split them in two?" Steven said, pretending to be horrified. "Gee, I don't think they're going to like that very much."

"Very funny, Steven," Jessica said. "You know what I mean. For instance, which one of us are *you* going to sponsor?"

Now Steven's horror was real. "Hey, I don't have enough money to sponsor either one of you."

"Oh, come now, Steven," Mr. Wakefield said. "If you put up a nickel a mile and the girls ride the whole way, that's only a total of three dollars. I think you can afford that for such a good cause."

"I guess," Steven muttered.

"Well, there you go, girls," Mrs. Wakefield said. "You have your first sponsor."

"How about you, Mom and Dad?" Elizabeth asked. "Are you going to sponsor both of us?"

"I think we can manage that," Mr. Wakefield said. "We'll put up a dollar a mile for each of you."

"Thanks!" Elizabeth said happily.

"But what about everyone else we know?" Jessica asked. "They might not sponsor both of us."

Mrs. Wakefield got up and began clearing the table. "They may or they may not, but that's a matter the two of you will have to work out yourselves."

After dinner, Lila Fowler and Ellen Riteman came over to study with Jessica. They followed her up to her room and the three girls immediately began talking about the bike-a-thon.

"I'm not going to have any trouble getting sponsors," Lila said. "I'm sure my father will pledge as much money as I ask him to." Lila's parents were divorced, and she lived with her father, who was very wealthy. He usually gave her anything she wanted, as a substitute for not being around very much.

"I'm not sure I'm going to enter the bike-a-thon," Ellen said, stretching out on Jessica's bed. "Thirty miles is such a long ride."

"Oh, don't be a baby," Jessica said. "You can ride that far."

"I *could*, if I wanted to," Ellen replied.

"Well, everybody is going to be riding," Jessica reminded Ellen. Then she giggled. "Even Lois Waller."

"Did you see what she was eating for lunch

today?" Ellen asked, sitting up straight on the bed.

"I *heard* it," Jessica answered, "when Bruce described the Walrus-menu to the entire lunchroom."

"Lois really ought to go on a diet," Lila said.

"I bet she can't ride one mile on a bicycle," Ellen added.

"Maybe she could go one mile an hour," Lila said. "At that rate it would take her more than one whole day to get to the finish line!"

Jessica stopped laughing when she noticed Elizabeth standing in the doorway. "Jessica, do you have my colored pencils?" Elizabeth asked.

"I think so," Jessica said, pointing toward the desk. "They're right over there, I think."

Elizabeth went over and picked up the pencils.

"Lizzie, you were having lunch with Lois today," Jessica said. "Is she really going to try to win the bike-a-thon?"

"Yes," Elizabeth replied. "And I think it's really terrific!" Before the girls could ask her any more questions, Elizabeth took the pencils and left the room.

Lila tossed her long brown hair over her shoulder. "I swear, Jessica, sometimes I wonder about that sister of yours."

Jessica agreed with Lila; she didn't think Elizabeth should hang around with so many of the unpopular girls. But all she said was, "You know Elizabeth. She always feels sorry for somebody."

Lila just shook her head.

Jessica wanted to change the subject. "I read in *SMASH!* magazine that a new Johnny Buck album will be out soon," she said.

Lila looked smug. "I already know all about it."

"You read the article, too?" Jessica asked.

"No. Better than that," Lila said in a mysterious tone.

"Tell us!" Ellen demanded.

"OK," Lila agreed happily. "Do you remember my uncle Seth? The one who works for a record company?"

Jessica and Ellen both nodded.

"Well, he works for the same company that handles Johnny Buck. And he promised me that as soon as the record is finished, even before it's shipped to the record stores, he'll send me a copy!"

"Fantastic!" Ellen said.

"When? When will you have it?" Jessica demanded.

"I'm not sure. But my uncle says it should be in a week or two," Lila answered, clearly satisfied by her friends' reactions.

"Can we come over and listen to it the second you get it?" Ellen asked.

Lila pretended to think about it.

"Come on, Lila, you've got to say yes," Ellen begged. "We love Johnny as much as you do!"

"It will be more fun for you to listen to it with us," Jessica added.

Finally Lila nodded. "OK, you can come over when I get it. We'll be the first ones in Sweet Valley to hear it," she added proudly.

"We might be the first in the country!" Jessica cried.

After Lila and Ellen went home, Jessica still didn't feel like studying. She wandered into Elizabeth's room.

"Hi, Lizzie," she said, plopping down on her sister's bed. "Do you want to go downstairs and see if there's any ice cream left?"

Elizabeth's tone was chilly. "No thanks."

"Why are you in such a bad mood?" Jessica asked.

Elizabeth put down the book she had been reading. "I heard what you guys said about Lois," she replied.

"Oh," Jessica said, "Lois Waller asks for it."

"That's not true!" Elizabeth exclaimed. "What Bruce did to her today was horrible."

"Come on, Elizabeth!" Jessica said. "People like Bruce are always going to give people like Lois a hard time. That's just the way things are."

"That's your opinion," Elizabeth said firmly. "It's not the way things have to be. Maybe one day Lois will give Bruce a hard time."

Jessica laughed. "That will be the day," she said.

"Hey, Waller," Bruce yelled. "I know you have a ton of stuff on your tray, but could you hurry it up?"

It was the next day, and everyone was standing in the cafeteria line. Elizabeth was near the end of the line. Bruce was right behind Lois, who was getting her lunch card stamped by the cashier.

Lois clutched her tray and at the same time tried to adjust her book bag, which was slipping off her arm. Elizabeth did not see quite how it happened, but as Bruce stepped up to the cashier, Lois dropped her bag. Bruce got his feet tangled in its straps, and the next thing Elizabeth knew, Bruce was sprawled on the ground, his tray upside down. Milk splashed all over the floor and all over Bruce, and bits of macaroni and cheese clung to his clothes.

Lois stood very still, a horrified look on her face.

"Oh, Bruce, I'm sorry," she whispered.

"I'll bet you are," Bruce said, his eyes blazing.

"No, really, it was an accident."

"Sure it was," Bruce said angrily, dabbing at his shirt with a milk-soaked napkin.

An eighth-grade lunchroom monitor, holding a mop and some towels, came up to Bruce. "Here, Patman, start cleaning this up so no one falls."

"Me?" Bruce said, outraged. "It was her fault," he added, pointing to Lois.

"I'll do it," Lois said, reaching for the mop.

"No, it's Patman's mess," the monitor insisted. "He'll clean it up. You just go sit down."

There was nothing for Lois to do but obey. While Bruce worked on cleaning up the mess, everyone in the lunchroom enjoyed the spectacle. It wasn't often that the great Bruce Patman was caught looking stupid.

Finally, the awful chore was finished. Bruce shoved the mop into a corner and stomped over to the table where his friends Charlie Cashman and Scott Joslin were sitting.

As he passed a group of eighth-graders, one of the boys called, "Hey, Patman, hope you enjoyed your trip." The boys sitting with him hooted with laughter. "Macaroni and cheese looks good on you, Bruce!" someone else called. "You should wear orange more often."

Again the whole group broke into laughter.

Bruce was furious. Usually, people didn't make fun of him. And he especially did not appreciate being ridiculed now. As Bruce slid into his seat, he muttered to his friends, "Not one word, or you'll be sorry."

Scott put up his hands. "Hey, we wouldn't say anything."

But Bruce noticed that Scott's lips were twitching. He was obviously having a hard time keeping the smile off of his face.

"Come on, Bruce. It was kind of funny," Charlie said. "You have to admit it."

"No, I don't. And she is going to get it," Bruce said fiercely.

"Who?" Scott asked.

"Who do you think?" Bruce said, turning an angry face toward his friend. "Lois Waller, that's who."

"What are you going to do to her?" Scott asked with interest.

Bruce's face was dark. "I don't know yet, but that girl was looking for trouble. And she's about to find it!"

Three

◆

"All right, everyone. Are we ready to start?" Elizabeth asked, raising her voice a little.

Amy Sutton, Julie Porter, and a few others who had recently joined the *Sixers*—including Patrick Morris—settled down for the weekly meeting of the newspaper staff.

Elizabeth studied her notes. "Patrick, you were going to cover the volleyball game."

"I did. We won. It was a great game, and I've got some really good quotes from the coach. I can have the story to you on Monday."

"Good." Elizabeth nodded her approval. "Julie, what about the Seventh-Grade Sing?"

"It's going to take place over the weekend," Julie told her. "I'll be there."

Elizabeth leaned back in her chair. "The next thing we need to talk about is the bike-a-thon."

"You know, that bike-a-thon is turning into a really big deal," Patrick said.

"Everyone's going crazy trying to find sponsors," Amy added.

Elizabeth's thoughts drifted to her own situation. Since the bike-a-thon had been announced two days ago, she hadn't had a single free minute to try to find sponsors. She wondered how Jessica was doing. The day before, Elizabeth had asked her twin if she had gotten any more people to sponsor her. All Jessica would say was, "You'll find out."

"Elizabeth, did you hear me?" Amy said.

"Sorry, Amy, what did you say?" Elizabeth asked.

"I said I thought we should assign a reporter to ask people how they're getting sponsors," Amy repeated.

"That's a great idea," Elizabeth said enthusiastically. "I'll bet there are some really interesting stories."

"Ken Matthews went over to the bus station and asked people to sign up," Patrick told her.

"And I heard that Grace Oliver asked people standing in line at Valley Cinema," Julie said.

"Julie," Elizabeth said, "why don't you talk to Ken and Grace and some of the other kids? See what you can come up with."

"All right." Julie made a note on her pad.

"Now, how should we cover the actual event?" Elizabeth asked. "I think we should definitely have one reporter at the finish line."

"And we should have reporters riding with the ones who have the most sponsors," Amy suggested.

"Right," Elizabeth agreed. "Then, when we write our stories, we can really give our readers an up-close look at what the bike-a-thon was like."

"It sounds as if we have our work cut out for us," Amy said.

"We do," Elizabeth agreed. "But it'll be worth it. This is going to be one of our best issues ever!"

* * *

On Saturday, Elizabeth realized that time was running out. She had to find more sponsors. The bike-a-thon was just a week away.

She called her grandmother, who told her that she would be glad to sponsor her for the same amount she had already promised Jessica—fifty cents a mile. Elizabeth wrote down her grand-mother's name on her pledge card. Then she wandered out to the patio where her mother was reading a book.

"Mom," Elizabeth said, pulling up a deck chair. "Can I call Aunt Helen?"

Mrs. Wakefield took off her sunglasses. "What for, Elizabeth?"

"I thought maybe she would sponsor me in the bike-a-thon."

"I guess you can," Mrs. Wakefield said slowly, "but I don't think you should spend more money on long-distance phone calls than you collect for the bike-a-thon."

"You're right," Elizabeth said with a sigh. "I've been so busy with the *Sixers* that I haven't had much time to find sponsors."

"I'm glad you and Jessica are both taking this seriously," Mrs. Wakefield said, "but no matter how few or how many pledges you get, I'm sure the PTA will be grateful.''

Elizabeth felt a little guilty about her mother's words of support. Of course she wanted to do the best she could to raise money for the PTA, but she wanted to win the bike, too. It seemed like Jessica had a better chance than she did. At least, she was spending more time finding sponsors.

As if reading her mind, Mrs. Wakefield asked, ''How's Jessica doing?''

''I don't know,'' Elizabeth said. ''She won't tell me.''

Jessica stood in the middle of Valley Mall. People were rushing past her. She felt very virtuous. She had gotten up early in the morning and had taken the bus out to the mall, all in an effort to get more pledges.

Originally her plan had been to get other people to help her get the signatures she needed. Jessica had caught Mr. Wakefield the day before as he was leaving for his office.

''Dad, you've got a lot of people working for you, right?'' she asked.

''Well, not all of them work *for* me. I'd say

working *with* me is a better description. Why do you ask?"

Jessica held out her pledge card. "Well, if you could just take this into your office and ask people to sponsor me—" she began.

Before she could finish her sentence, Mr. Wakefield was shaking his head. "Sorry, Jess. I think this bike-a-thon is a good idea, but I'm not going to find sponsors for you."

"Maybe I could come down to the office and talk to them myself," Jessica suggested.

"I don't think so." Mr. Wakefield put his hand on his daughter's shoulder. "People might feel like they're being put on the spot, and I don't want to put that kind of pressure on them."

"Oh, Dad." Jessica groaned.

"I admire your industriousness, but I think it would be better if you find sponsors without my help. Just remember what's important, Jessica— not how many sponsors you get, but the fact that you're participating."

"Sure," Jessica told her father. *But the most important thing is winning the mountain bike*, she added to herself.

After her father turned her down, she tried to

get Steven to ask his high school friends to sponsor her. When he refused, the only other idea she came up with was going to the mall.

Now she found herself in the difficult position of having to ask strangers to sponsor her. She had already asked countless passersby, and had only gotten two new pledges as a result. The morning wasn't turning out at all the way she had hoped. She was just about to give up when she saw Bruce Patman walking by the bookstore. She casually sauntered over to him and said, "Hi, Bruce."

"Oh, hi, Jessica." He looked at the pledge card in her hand. "Don't tell me you're here trying to get sponsors?"

"Yeah. You, too?"

"No way," Bruce said. "I haven't even decided if I'm going to ride in it yet."

Bruce suddenly pointed in the direction of the fudge store. "Hey, look. There goes Lois Waller, getting something to feed her face, as usual. I don't know anyone who eats as much as she does." His gaze followed Lois into the candy store. "Lois hasn't heard the last from me."

Jessica knew better than to ask how Bruce was

planning to get back at Lois. She knew she would find out soon enough.

When Jessica got home, she peeked into Elizabeth's room. Her sister was sitting at her desk, working.

"What are you doing?" Jessica asked.

"Figuring out how much money I'll make on the bike-a-thon," Elizabeth told her.

"How many sponsors do you have so far?" Jessica asked, flinging herself down on Elizabeth's bed.

"Not many. Dad, Mom, Grandma, and of course, Steven's huge contribution." Elizabeth giggled.

"I'm doing a little better than that, but not much," Jessica complained. She described her morning at the mall.

"Wow, Jess, I'm impressed," Elizabeth said. "You've put a lot more effort into this than I have."

"I guess so," Jessica said sadly. "But I don't think it matters. Neither one of us has enough sponsors to win that bike."

"I can't wait until the next basketball game,"

Ellen said. It was after school on Monday, and a group of Unicorns were walking home together.

"Yeah, me, too," Lila grumbled. "Maybe that will get everyone to stop talking about this stupid bike-a-thon."

"I'm not riding in it," Janet Howell announced. Janet was an eighth-grader and the president of the Unicorn Club.

"You're not?" Jessica asked, surprised.

"Bike thirty miles in the hot sun?" Janet exclaimed. "No way!"

Ellen and Lila looked at each other. "I can't think of any reason we have to ride in it, either," Lila said thoughtfully.

"You're right," Jessica said. The more she thought about it, the more awful the idea of a thirty-mile bike ride seemed. Especially now that she knew she had no chance of winning the bicycle.

"Let's all drop out then," Lila said.

"Sounds good to me," Ellen agreed.

All three of the girls looked at Jessica. "What about you, Jessica?" Lila asked.

"Well, count me out, too," Jessica said.

Janet smiled at her. "Great. The Unicorns should stick together. We'll think of something really fun to do that day." Jessica smiled back at her, but she got a sinking feeling in her stomach. *She* didn't mind quitting the bike-a-thon, but she knew her parents would be disappointed in her.

You're just going to have to make sure they don't find out, Jessica told herself. Because Jessica was sure about one thing: If the rest of the Unicorns were not going to be in the bike-a-thon, neither was she.

Four

◇

On Tuesday morning before school started, Elizabeth saw Lois Waller standing outside of their homeroom.

"Hi, Lois," Elizabeth said, walking over to her.

Lois brushed a strand of hair out of her eyes. "Hi, Elizabeth."

The two girls walked into the classroom together. Lois began to chatter about the bike-a-thon. Elizabeth had never seen her so excited.

When the first bell rang, Mr. Davis clapped his hands to get the class's attention. "Boys and girls, as you know, the bike-a-thon will take place this Saturday. Friday is the last day for you to hand in your pledge cards. Does anyone want to tell me how many sponsors they've signed up?"

Winston Egbert raised his hand. "I've got twelve."

"Very good," Mr. Davis said approvingly.

Elizabeth and Jessica exchanged glances. Both doubted they had that many sponsors *between* them.

A few more reported their results. Amy Sutton had nine names on her pledge card, and Ken Matthews had thirteen.

"Thirteen," Mr. Davis said. "Very good. Does anyone have more than thirteen?"

Lois Waller slowly raised her hand.

"Yes, Lois?"

"I've got twenty-three names," she said quietly.

The classroom buzzed.

"Twenty-three?" Mr. Davis repeated, clearly surprised.

"That's right," Lois said. She held up her pledge card. Attached to it was an extra sheet of paper and it was filled with names.

"That's terrific, Lois. It looks as though you're going to be the class leader," Mr. Davis said.

When homeroom was over, just about everyone in class went over to Lois to congratulate her and find out how she had gathered so many names.

"First, I asked all my relatives," she said.

"You must have a big family," Patrick commented.

"I do. But I also asked my neighbors and put pledge cards in a couple of stores in my neighborhood. Every day I went in to check who'd signed up. I called each person to explain the rules and to make sure that they were actually going to pledge."

Winston Egbert whistled. "Wow, you're really well organized, Lois."

Lois shrugged. "I guess so."

"You did a great job," Elizabeth said, smiling. "I hope you win."

It didn't take long for the news of Lois's successful pledge drive to spread around the school. All morning, her classmates congratulated her. No one had as many sponsors as she did. When Elizabeth spotted Lois at lunchtime, she looked dazed and excited by all the attention.

"Come sit with us," Elizabeth called, moving over to make room for Lois. Amy and Julie sat across the table.

"Wow, what a morning. I didn't think that

many kids were interested in the bike-a-thon!" Lois told them.

"Oh, they are," Elizabeth said. "That's why we're doing so many stories about it in the *Sixers*."

"It certainly looks like you're going to win that bike," Julie commented.

"I hope so." Lois gazed off into space. "I really would love to own it."

"Don't just think about how many sponsors you have. How far you can ride counts, too," Amy reminded Lois.

A worried look crossed Lois's face. "I don't know how far I can ride," she said, "but I'm sure going to try to make it to the end."

In another corner of the lunchroom, Scott Joslin was sitting with Bruce Patman.

"I guess you've heard the news," Scott said.

"What news?" Bruce asked.

"About your old pal Lois."

Bruce pushed his plate aside. "What about her?"

"She's got twenty-three sponsors for the bike-a-thon."

"You're kidding," Bruce said.

"I'm not," Scott replied.

"Well, she doesn't have a chance of winning if I decide to enter," Bruce said.

"But I thought you decided not to," Scott said.

"I guess I could always change my mind," Bruce replied. "This contest must mean a lot to Lois . . ."

"Sure. Why else would she have gone to the trouble of getting all those sponsors?"

Bruce leaned back in his chair. "You know, Lois made me the laughingstock of the whole school."

Scott chuckled. "Yeah, all that macaroni and cheese—"

"Scott . . ." Bruce said angrily.

"OK, OK, but it was funny."

A tense look appeared on Bruce's face. "Well, if I were Lois Waller, I wouldn't count on winning that bike quite yet. This just might be payback time for old Lois."

By suppertime, Bruce had figured out what he was going to do. The Patmans were just finishing their dinner. On warm evenings like this, the family ate outside on their well-tended terrace.

Bruce waited until the housekeeper had served their dessert. Then he said casually to his parents, "You know we're having a fund raiser at school. There's going to be a bike-a-thon, and all the money raised is going to be used to buy VCRs and instructional video tapes for the library."

"That's nice, dear," Mrs. Patman said.

"Are you going to participate, Bruce?" his father asked.

"Well, I've been thinking about it. Would you sponsor me?"

"Of course," his father agreed readily.

Bruce pulled a pledge card from his pants pocket.

Mr. Patman took the card and looked it over. "We have to pledge a certain amount per mile, I see."

"That's right," Bruce said.

"How much are other people pledging?" Mr. Patman asked.

Bruce was deliberately vague. "I'm not sure. But I thought you and Mom could pledge about ten dollars a mile. Each."

"That comes to twenty dollars a mile," Mr. Patman said. "And if you ride the whole thirty miles . . ."

"That would be six hundred dollars," Bruce finished for him.

Mrs. Patman peered at her son over her coffee cup. "That's quite a bit of money, Bruce."

"Oh, I know it is, but it's for a good cause."

"I suppose there's no question you'll ride the whole way?" Mr. Patman asked.

"Not with that great bike you gave me. I could probably go sixty miles on that."

Mr. and Mrs. Patman exchanged glances. "I suppose it would be all right," Mrs. Patman said, looking pleased by her son's confidence.

"I agree," Mr. Patman said, returning the card to Bruce. "I'm glad to see you're taking part in such a good cause."

"Oh, uh, I'm glad you approve, Dad." But Bruce's mind was already on how he was going to get even with Lois Waller.

"So are you girls all ready for Saturday?" Mr. Wakefield asked that evening.

Jessica, who was leafing through a fashion magazine, didn't answer.

"I guess so," Elizabeth said.

"You don't sound very enthusiastic, dear," Mrs. Wakefield said.

"Oh, I guess I'm more concerned about covering the story for the *Sixers*."

"But you're still going to ride, aren't you?" her father asked.

"Yes. I think I'm going to ride with the person who has the most sponsors, Lois Waller."

"What about you, Jessica?" Mrs. Wakefield said.

Jessica glanced up, hoping she didn't look too guilty. This would be a perfect opportunity to tell her parents she was dropping out of the bike-a-thon, but she just did not have the courage to say it.

"I'm as ready as I'll ever be," she responded. That was the truth at least.

A little while later, as the twins were brushing their teeth side by side in the bathroom they shared, Jessica had a thought. Maybe Elizabeth would help her get out of the bike-a-thon.

Rinsing off her toothbrush, Jessica said, "Lizzie, I need your help."

Elizabeth looked at her sister suspiciously. "With what?" she asked.

Jessica laughed. "Don't get upset, Elizabeth."

Elizabeth waited to see what was coming next.

"It's just that I don't think I want to ride in the bike-a-thon anymore."

Elizabeth was surprised. "But you tried so hard to find sponsors," she said.

"And I didn't do so well, did I? It's going to be hot and tiring, and I know I'm not going to win that bike."

Elizabeth stuck her toothbrush back in the rack. "Winning the bike isn't everything, you know. Think about the PTA contribution."

"What do you think Mom and Dad will say?"

"I don't think they'll be too happy, Jess." Elizabeth turned to walk into her own room.

"But maybe if you help me explain . . ."

Elizabeth continued into her room, and Jessica followed. "They'd take it better if it came from you," Jessica pleaded.

Elizabeth climbed into bed. "Sorry, Jessica, I can't do it," she said.

"Why not?" Jessica demanded.

"Because it's just a couple of hours of your time, and it's for a good cause. I think you're being selfish."

Jessica could see that she was not going to get anywhere with Elizabeth. She should have known better. Elizabeth would never understand that Jessica and her friends had decided that riding in the bike-a-thon wasn't worth it.

"All right, don't help me," she said, stomping back to her own room. She pulled her covers off her bed and got in.

From Elizabeth's room, she heard her sister call her name.

"What?" Jessica called back.

"Are you going to ride or not?"

"I don't know," Jessica said. To herself, she added, "Not if I can help it."

Five

◇

Bruce Patman was sure that he would win the bike-a-thon, no matter how many sponsors Lois Waller had. The way he figured it, Lois couldn't possibly have six hundred dollars worth of pledges. Even if she did, there was no way she could ride the whole race. Just thinking about Lois huffing and puffing through thirty miles of bike trail was enough to bring a smile to his lips. *If she goes ten miles, it'll be a miracle*, he thought.

The night before, he had been thinking about the best way to give Lois the bad news. He had decided he would tell her in the school yard, first thing. But now, as he saw Lois surrounded by a couple of classmates who were congratulating her on all of her sponsors, he decided to wait. The happier Lois Waller was about winning, the worse she would feel when he finally told her that she was going to be beaten—by him.

Lois caught up with Elizabeth on her way to their English class, and pulled her aside.

"What's wrong, Lois?" Elizabeth asked when she saw the worried look on Lois's face.

"Every time I turn around today, Bruce Patman is looking at me," Lois said in a low voice.

Elizabeth glanced over her shoulder. Sure enough, there was Bruce leaning against a locker, staring at Lois. "I see what you mean," she said.

"I think he's planning something," Lois said.

"He does look like he has something up his sleeve," Elizabeth said. "I wonder what it could be."

"It could be anything. Maybe he's planning to yell out everything I've got on my tray at lunch."

"No," Elizabeth replied. "I don't think he'll try that again."

"Well, I know he hasn't forgiven me for tripping him on my book bag. It really was just an accident, and I told him that over and over."

"I know." Elizabeth looked at Lois with sympathy.

"I wish Bruce would believe me. He can't seem to stop thinking about it."

Elizabeth didn't know what to say. But she knew that Lois had reason to be concerned. Bruce Patman didn't forgive easily, and he certainly didn't forget. There was no telling what he was up to.

Lois spent a nervous lunch period waiting to see what Bruce would do. She made sure that all she had on her tray was a salad and a plate of Jell-O. Let Bruce inform everyone in the cafeteria of *that* if he wanted to!

Bruce didn't say a word during lunch, but Lois could feel his eyes on her as she ate. She was surprised when the afternoon passed without any trouble from him.

Lois had just put her books in her locker and was heading out the main door, when she felt a hand on her shoulder. Whirling around, she found herself staring straight into the eyes of Bruce Patman.

"What do you want?" she asked nervously.

"I just want to give you some news," Bruce said.

"Well, I don't want any news from you," Lois replied, turning back toward the door.

Bruce danced around in front of her. "But it's about the bike-a-thon. You want to hear news about that, don't you?"

Lois could not get past Bruce. "OK. What's your big news?" she asked.

"You're going to lose, Lois," Bruce said gleefully. "You haven't got a chance of winning that bike."

"Why not?" Lois asked indignantly.

Bruce pulled his pledge card from his pocket and stuck it in her hands. "Here's why."

"Your parents each pledged ten dollars a mile!" Lois exclaimed.

"Brilliant, Lois! And since you read so well, I guess you can do arithmetic, too."

Lois did a quick multiplication in her head. The figure six hundred dollars came immediately to mind. Her heart sank.

"Aren't you going to say something, Walrus?" Bruce folded his arms across his chest and smiled with satisfaction.

Lois could feel tears forming behind her eyes, but she was determined not to let Bruce see her cry. "This doesn't mean anything," she said, shoving the card back at him.

"Admit it, I've got this bike-a-thon all wrapped up," Bruce taunted.

Whirling around, Lois hurried through the door. She was starting to cry, and she didn't want Bruce to see. She could hear him laughing behind her. Her only thought was to get away from him, to get away from school. She stumbled through the school yard, until a hand on her arm stopped her. At first she thought it was Bruce. But when she looked up, Lois saw it was Elizabeth. Amy and Julie were standing next to her.

"Lois, what happened?" Elizabeth asked. "Did Bruce finally say something to you?"

Lois nodded. She couldn't find the words to speak.

"We were just going over to the Dairi Burger for a soda," Elizabeth said. "Why don't you come with us? You can fill us in on the whole story when we get there."

"Come on, Lois," Amy said. "Maybe we can think of some way to get back at that creep."

The place was packed as usual, but the girls found a small table in a corner. They pushed their way through the crowd and took the seats before a group of older girls could get to them. Then they took turns going up to the counter and giving their orders.

When they were all seated with their food, Lois quickly filled them in on Bruce's big pledges for the bike-a-thon. She finished by saying, "I don't have a chance."

"You're not going to let Bruce get away with this, are you?" Amy asked.

"Well, I have to ride, of course. I owe it to my sponsors and to the school. But it's hard to get really excited about it, knowing Bruce is going to win anyway."

"I can't believe Bruce!" Julie exclaimed. "The only reason *he* wants that bike is because he knows *you* want it."

"Now he'll have two really great bikes." Lois sighed.

"Maybe not," Elizabeth said.

"What do you mean?" Amy asked.

"Lois, do you have your pledge card with you?"

"Sure," she said, pulling it out of her book bag.

"Great. Give me a pencil and a piece of paper."

"Elizabeth, what are you doing?" Amy asked.

"You'll see!"

After a few moments of careful calculating, Elizabeth turned to Lois with a smile on her face.

"What?" Lois demanded. "What did you find out?"

Elizabeth handed her the piece of paper. While Lois was scanning it, Elizabeth said, "Most of your pledges are for small amounts, but you have a ton of them."

Now Lois's eyes were shining. She waved the piece of paper in front of Amy and Julie. "Added all together, they come to eighteen dollars and fifty cents per mile!"

"That's almost as much as Bruce will make," Amy said with excitement.

"Yes, but eighteen-fifty per mile still isn't twenty dollars," Julie said.

"No, it isn't," Lois agreed cheerfully.

Julie gave her a curious look. "You don't seem too upset by that fact."

"I'm not. Because it's close enough. With a few more pledges, I could catch up to Bruce."

"Then you and Bruce would both be riding for twenty dollars a mile," Amy said.

"I've got a day and a half left before I have to turn in my pledge card. I intend to spend the entire time making sure that's just what happens."

"But, Lois, practically everyone in town has been asked by now," Julie reminded her.

"I can't believe everyone is taken," Lois said. "Believe me, I'll find a few who haven't been asked yet."

"I believe you," Elizabeth said, "but even if you get as much money as Bruce, you'd still have to ride the whole way to win. Do you think you can make it? There's no question that Bruce can, with that great bike of his."

A determined look came over Lois's face. "Don't worry, Elizabeth. After I've gone to all this trouble, I'm going to ride as hard and as long as I possibly can. Maybe I won't go the whole thirty miles, but by the time I'm done, Bruce Patman will think twice about bugging me again!"

Lois left the Dairi Burger filled with enthusiasm. If Bruce Patman thought she was going to give in so easily, he was crazy. The problem was she couldn't think of any more people available to sponsor her. She had already gotten her family, all her friends, and practically her whole neighborhood.

Her steps began to slow. What if Julie was

right? Maybe there was no one left in town who had not already been asked.

Since the retirement home where her mother worked was on the way home, Lois stopped in to say hello before starting her homework. She waved to Mrs. Newman, the woman at the front desk, before going off to find her mother, who was usually in the lounge taking blood pressure and checking pulses this time of day.

"Hi, sweetie," Mrs. Waller said when Lois walked into the room. She was sitting with a friendly woman named Mrs. Williams.

"Hi, Mom. Hi, Mrs. Williams," Lois said politely.

"Hello, Lois," Mrs. Williams said. "It's so nice to see you, dear. How was school today?"

Lois shrugged. "All right, I guess."

"Are you sure?" Mrs. Waller asked.

Suddenly, Lois couldn't keep the day's events inside. "I was sure I was going to win the bike-a-thon," she said angrily. "But now Bruce Patman is ruining everything!"

"What's a bike-a-thon?" Mrs. Williams asked.

Lois filled her in on the project. She also told them about Bruce. "Bruce is just angry because I accidentally tripped him. He doesn't care at all about winning the bike, *or* raising money for the library."

"I understand how you feel, but remember, you're still helping out your school, whether or not you win the bike," Mrs. Waller said.

"I know. But I really wanted that bike so that I could start my paper route." Lois sighed. "If I could only find a few more sponsors I'd at least have a *chance* of winning, but I just can't think of anyone else to ask."

"Well, you haven't asked *me* yet," Mrs. Williams said with a twinkle in her eye.

"Oh, no," Mrs. Waller interrupted. "I told Lois when this whole thing started that she couldn't possibly bother the people who live here."

Mrs. Williams waved away her objections. "Don't be silly. It would make me feel good to know that I'm helping young people. Just because I'm old doesn't mean I have no interest in what's happening in the outside world."

Lois looked hopefully at her mother.

"All right," Mrs. Waller said. "I give in! If you insist, Lily, you can be one of Lois's sponsors." Then she turned to Lois. "But I don't want you asking anyone else, Lois. Others may not be as generous as Mrs. Williams, and we don't want to make anyone feel uncomfortable. Now you'll have to excuse me. I have to finish my rounds."

Mrs. Waller patted her daughter on the arm and walked away, taking all of Lois's high hopes with her. For one moment she had thought that maybe the people who lived at the retirement home were the key to winning the bike-a-thon. But her mother was probably right. It wasn't very nice to bother them.

Mrs. Williams was gazing thoughtfully into space. "Lois," she said, "I don't like to get in between young people and their parents, but I think your mother has made a mistake."

"What do you mean?" Lois asked.

"She assumes that the residents of the retirement home would consider backing you in the bike-a-thon a nuisance."

"Wouldn't they?"

"Not in my opinion. It gets boring around here. Rooting you on in the bike-a-thon, hearing about how you did—I'm sure many people here would enjoy that."

"Do you really? But how could I ask them when my mother told me not to bother anyone?"

Mrs. Williams smiled. "You don't have to bother anyone. I bother people around here all the time."

"You mean . . . ?" Lois began.

"Where's that pledge card?" Mrs. Williams cut in.

Lois pulled the card out of her book bag and handed it to Mrs. Williams. "Are you sure you want to do this?"

"I can't force anyone to pledge, Lois, but I'm certain there will be a number of people wanting to contribute." Determination strengthened her voice. "We're going to show that Bruce Patman what's what!"

Six

◇

Elizabeth woke up early on the morning of the bike-a-thon. She smiled, remembering how excited Lois had been the day before, when she had turned in her pledge card to Mr. Davis. Lois had explained to Elizabeth how she had found a few new sponsors at the retirement home where her mother worked. She would now be riding for almost twenty-one dollars a mile—more than Bruce! If she could just go the whole distance, she would beat him.

"Morning, Lizzie." Jessica stuck her head inside the door. "Breakfast is ready. And it's a good one. Mom said we'll need extra energy today, so she's making waffles and bacon.''

"Thanks, Jess. Ready for the bike-a-thon?" Elizabeth asked her twin with a smile. Jessica frowned in response.

While Elizabeth showered, Jessica sat on her bed and thought about the bike-a-thon. She was still trying to figure out a way to get out of it. The phone interrupted her thoughts. "I'll get it," she called out, and then picked up the phone in the hallway.

"Jessica!" Lila's voice came bubbling through the receiver. "It's here!"

"What's here?" Jessica said.

"The new Johnny Buck album. It's called 'Pass the Buck.' "

Jessica screamed. "When did you get it?"

"It came special delivery this morning. Ellen and Janet are coming over this afternoon to listen to it."

"This afternoon? But the bike-a-thon is this afternoon!"

"I thought we all decided we weren't going to be in that stupid thing."

"I know. It's just that I haven't exactly told my parents yet."

"Well, you'd better hurry up," Lila said. "There's no way we're going to wait another day to hear this album. Of course, if you don't care . . ." Lila's voice trailed off.

"No, I want to hear it today with the rest of you."

"Everyone else will be here at one o'clock," Lila informed her. "I've asked a few boys over, too."

"Boys!" Jessica said. "Who?"

"Scott Joslin, for one. He's not riding. And a couple of other seventh-graders. But we're not going to wait around for you."

"All right, I get the message," Jessica said. "I'll be there by one."

After she hung up the phone, Jessica stood in the hallway, thinking. There was no way she was going to miss out on hearing that album, especially since there were going to be boys at the party. An idea began forming in her head. It wouldn't be easy, but it just might work.

Yes, I'm sure it will, she thought to herself as she walked downstairs and out the front door.

Elizabeth was finishing her second waffle when Jessica re-entered the house and sat down at the kitchen table.

"Where have you been?" Mrs. Wakefield asked.

"Oh, I had something to do," Jessica said mysteriously.

"Well, you'd better get something in your stomach or you won't have the energy to ride," Mr. Wakefield said.

"Yeah, you'd better hurry," Steven added, spearing another waffle, "or the food will be all gone."

Jessica shot him a dirty look. "I'm surprised there's any left now."

"Which one of you girls is going to win that mountain bike?" Mr. Wakefield asked with a grin.

"Very funny, Dad," Jessica said.

"I hope it's going to be Lois Waller," Elizabeth replied. "She's worked so hard to get her pledges. And Bruce Patman has been giving her a hard time, so she deserves to win." She filled her parents in on all the trouble that Bruce had been causing.

"Oh, Lizzie, you're just prejudiced against Bruce," Jessica said.

"And *you're* sticking up for him because you think he's cute." Elizabeth could never figure out why her sister liked Bruce.

"Has my little sister got a boyfriend?" Steven asked, raising an eyebrow at Jessica.

"No, I have not," Jessica said. "I just think everyone is unfair to Bruce."

"Why's that?" Mrs. Wakefield asked.

"Just because he's cute and rich, some people don't like him," she answered, looking over at Elizabeth. "But Bruce is honest. He says what he thinks. Lois Waller *is* too fat. If she hates being teased so much, she can lose some weight."

Mrs. Wakefield looked surprised. "Jessica, what a cruel thing to say."

"Well, it's true," Jessica said, licking a drop of syrup off her finger.

"Beauty is as beauty does," her father remarked.

Jessica looked puzzled.

"Your father means you can't judge people by appearances," Mrs. Wakefield explained.

"Oh, I know that," Jessica said.

Mr. Wakefield pushed himself away from the table. "If you will all excuse me, I think I'll go check the bikes. I want to make sure you girls have plenty of air in your tires."

"Good idea, Dad," Jessica said. "We'll go with you." This was the moment she had been waiting for.

The twins and Mr. Wakefield trooped outside. Steven decided to follow them.

Elizabeth and Jessica wheeled their bikes onto the driveway. Elizabeth's moved smoothly, but the rim of one of Jessica's wheels scraped loudly against the ground.

"Jessica," Mr. Wakefield said, noticing the irregular motion of her tire, "is there something wrong with your bike?"

Jessica tried to look concerned. "I think there is, Dad."

Taking the bike from her, Mr. Wakefield inspected it closely. "Looks like you have a flat," he said. "I wonder how that happened."

Jessica studied a crack in the driveway.

"I hope it just needs air and doesn't have a leak," Mr. Wakefield said.

"If there's a leak, does that mean I can't ride?" Jessica asked, trying not to sound too eager. Elizabeth gave her a curious look.

Before Mr. Wakefield could answer, Steven said, "Let me see it, Dad."

Steven wheeled the bike over to the grass and then disappeared into the house.

Mrs. Wakefield joined the family out on the driveway. "What's wrong, Ned?"

"Jessica's tire is flat," Mr. Wakefield answered her.

"Don't worry, I can fix it," Steven said, reappearing with the bicycle pump.

Jessica's face fell. Why did Steven have to be so handy all of a sudden?

It didn't take him long. In just a few minutes, he had the tire pumped up. "It's strange, but there doesn't seem to be a hole in it," he said, handing the bike over to Jessica. "It's as good as new now."

"Thanks, Steven. But what if it blows out again during the race? I could fly over a bump and be thrown off or something!"

Mrs. Wakefield looked concerned. "Do you think that's possible?"

Mr. Wakefield wheeled the bike back and forth. "It seems fine to me," he said.

"But, Mom, just because it's all right now . . ."

"Jessica, is there some reason you don't want to be in this bike-a-thon?" Mrs. Wakefield asked.

Jessica could feel her face getting red.

"Jessica?" her mother said.

"Well, some of the kids are going over to Lila's to listen to the new Johnny Buck album."

Before she'd even finished her sentence, Mrs. Wakefield was shaking her head. "You can go after the race if you want, but you have made a commitment that your father and I expect you to keep."

"Besides," Steven added, "I spent a lot of time and effort fixing that bike of yours."

"Oh, sure." Jessica glared at him. "Two whole seconds. Thanks for coming to my rescue."

Steven gave a little bow. "My pleasure."

"If I have to ride, then I'd better go up and change," Jessica said crossly.

"That's a good idea," her mother agreed.

"I knew they'd never understand," Jessica muttered to herself as she stomped up the stairs to her room.

After checking out her bike, Elizabeth went upstairs, looking for Jessica. She knew how her sister felt about missing the afternoon at Lila's. She thought she would try and cheer her up a little.

She expected to find a grumpy Jessica complaining about how unfair her life was. Instead, she found a smiling Jessica preening in front of the mirror—wearing a new pair of shorts and a Johnny Buck T-shirt.

"Why are you wearing your best shorts, Jess?" Elizabeth asked. "You're going to get them all messed up. Thirty miles is a long ride, you know, and we might be going through puddles or mud or something."

Jessica giggled. "Well, I won't be going thirty miles so I don't have to worry."

"You won't?"

"Nope. I'm not going to be riding long enough to get even a little speck of dirt on my new shorts."

Elizabeth sat down on the bed. "What are you up to, Jess?"

"Mom said I had to ride. But she didn't say I had to ride *the whole way*. I'll go a couple of miles, and then I'll quit. There will be plenty of time to get to Lila's before one o'clock," she added, a satisfied smile on her face.

"Oh, Jessica," Elizabeth groaned. "I don't think that's exactly what Mom and Dad had in mind."

"Look, Elizabeth, I'm doing just what they said I could. First I'm riding, then I'm going over to Lila's." She glanced over at her sister. "You're not thinking of telling them I'm not planning to ride the full thirty miles, are you?"

Elizabeth shook her head. "You know I wouldn't. Besides, I guess you are *technically* staying within the rules."

Jessica grinned at her sister. "I know I am. Now let's go over to that bike-a-thon. The sooner I get started, the sooner I can leave!"

"I guess we'd better go register," Elizabeth said, glancing at her watch and then at the huge crowd of kids that had collected. "It's almost twelve."

"I'll be there in a second," Jessica said. She had noticed Bruce Patman standing off by himself near the fence.

Elizabeth shrugged. "All right." She started to wheel her bike away.

Jessica put the kickstand down on her bike and walked over to Bruce, who was adjusting his seat.

"Hi, Bruce."

Bruce barely looked up. "Hi, Jessica."

Jessica cleared her throat. Bruce Patman always made her nervous, but she was determined not to let it show. "Remember that new Johnny Buck album I told you about?"

"The one Lila's uncle was sending her?"

"That's right. It came this morning by special delivery and a bunch of kids are going over later to listen to it. Scott and Charlie will both be there."

Bruce began to look interested. "What time is all this happening?"

"About one," Jessica said eagerly.

"Well, I plan to finish the race pretty fast, but I don't know if I can get there that soon. After all, the race *is* thirty miles."

Jessica didn't feel like explaining that she wasn't going to be riding the whole way. "Why don't you come over as soon as you're finished, then? I'm sure we'll still be there."

"I guess I can make it sometime this afternoon."

"Great," Jessica said enthusiastically. "And, Bruce?"

"What?"

"I hope you win." Jessica shyly looked down at the ground.

"I will," Bruce said confidently. "The first thing I'm going to do is pass old Lois huffing and puffing along, and then I'm going to speed to the finish line."

"And I'll be right behind you," Amy Sutton said, coming up to Bruce and Jessica.

Bruce gave Amy a cold stare. "What are you talking about?"

"I'm covering the bike-a-thon for the *Sixers*.

The two front-runners are going to have reporters with them, and I'm assigned to you."

Bruce looked at Amy's heavy three-speed bike.
"You think you're going to keep up with me on
that thing?" he asked with disdain.

"Good luck, Amy," Jessica said, giggling.

Amy's expression turned serious. "I'm going
to try my best," she said.

"Well, you can do whatever you want," Bruce
said. "It's a free country. But I'll tell you one
thing, I'm not going to wait around for you.
You'll be eating my dust, Amy."

Amy went back to where Elizabeth was standing with Lois. "Bruce is not going to make this
easy for me," she told Elizabeth.

"I know," Elizabeth said. "Keep up with him
as long as you can. That's all you can do."

"I guess keeping up with me won't be that
much of a problem, Elizabeth," Lois said with a
sigh.

Elizabeth looked at her. This was the first time
she had ever seen Lois out of her school clothes,
and she was surprised to note that in a T-shirt
and shorts, Lois didn't look so heavy.

"You never know, Lois. We might finish before Bruce!"

"I don't know about that, Elizabeth. Just look at him. His bike is great, and he really looks like he's in shape."

"Come on, Lois, don't lose confidence now!" Elizabeth exclaimed.

"I'm not," Lois said, "but let's face it. It's going to take a lot to beat Bruce Patman!"

Seven

◇

The race was about to begin. All the riders were wearing white bike helmets with "Sweet Valley Bike-a-Thon" printed on the front. The helmets were part of the official bike-a-thon kit that each rider had received.

Also in the kit was a mileage card that the riders were to carry with them. The numbers one through thirty were printed on the green card. Parents were stationed at check-out points at each mile along the route, and as the riders passed, they would have their cards punched. The mileage card would be the official record of how far each rider had gone.

Mr. Clark, the principal, picked up a bullhorn. "Attention, everybody," he boomed. "First," he began, "I would like to congratulate all of you in advance. No matter how far you ride today, you have all done a fine job of collecting sponsors. You can be proud of yourselves for helping your school raise money for a worthy cause."

A cheer went up from the crowd.

Mr. Clark continued. "When I blow the whistle, the race will begin. Don't rush to get away from the starting line first. Remember, slow and steady wins the race."

"Slow and steady," repeated Lois, who was poised on her bike, next to Elizabeth.

"Good luck to all of you," the principal continued. "At the count of three you may begin. One, two . . ."

Elizabeth knew that Mr. Clark must have blown the whistle, but she didn't hear it. The sound of dozens of bicycles taking off drowned out the sound.

Despite the principal's plea to take their time getting started, all the riders tried to push toward the head of the group. Bruce Patman was almost the first one to pull away, with Amy pedaling close behind him.

For the first half mile, the huge group stayed close together, but then it began thinning out. The faster riders took a big lead, while the rest tried to keep up. Lois, with Elizabeth at her side, was bringing up the rear.

Elizabeth couldn't remember when she had ever ridden at such a snail's pace. Her legs seemed to be going in slow motion. She glanced over at Lois, who was rhythmically riding along. Lois didn't seem too concerned that they were falling farther and farther behind.

"How are you doing?" Elizabeth called to her.

Lois smiled. "OK. We're almost to the first checkpoint." She pointed at a small group of parents punching cards.

One down and twenty-nine to go, Elizabeth thought. It was going to be a long afternoon.

Elizabeth was right. It was long, but it was not quite as boring as Elizabeth suspected. The bike-a-thon organizers had planned an interesting route for the riders. After they pulled away from the school yard, the riders followed the bike path into a large park. The overhanging tree branches made a leafy arc to ride under, and flowers dotted the sides of the path.

By the fifth mile of the course, the riders were

out of the park and following a trail that went along wooded, scenic foothills. Sea gulls flew overhead, swooping and darting through the sky.

Some of the racers began to drop out at about the seventh mile. It was getting hot, and although water was available at each of the checkpoints, a lot of riders were tired and overheated. Elizabeth wondered if Jessica was still in the race, but she knew that if her sister had dropped out, it wasn't the heat that had gotten to her. Johnny Buck fever would be more like it.

At the ten-mile checkpoint, Lois got off her bike. After getting her card punched she grabbed a cup of water and gulped it down.

"How are you holding up, Lois?" Elizabeth asked, dismounting and coming over to the table where pitchers of water and paper cups were set out.

"I'm getting tired," Lois admitted.

"We've only gone a third of the course," Elizabeth said, reaching for the water.

"I know."

"You're not going to stop now, are you?"

"No way!" A new determination crept into Lois's voice. "Let's get back on our bikes."

"All *right!*" Elizabeth said.

The girls were still at the tail end of the pack, but they kept plugging away. Fifteen miles went by, then twenty.

"You're doing great, Lois," Elizabeth called.

By now Lois was so tired, she could barely answer. She just nodded and kept pumping her legs, around and around.

Elizabeth looked at her worriedly. Sweat glistened on Lois's brow, and her breathing was heavy. As they rode the twenty-first mile, Elizabeth asked if she wanted to rest.

"I don't want to rest. I want to stop."

"Really?"

"I don't think I can go much farther, Elizabeth," Lois told her.

Elizabeth wasn't sure she could make the whole thirty miles either, so she could imagine how Lois must be feeling.

"Maybe I'll go just a little while longer," Lois said.

"All right, but you've really pushed yourself. When you've gone as far as you can, we'll both stop."

After the twenty-second-mile checkpoint, Lois got off her bike and fell onto the grass. "That's it, Elizabeth. My legs feel like lead. There's no way I can go another mile."

Elizabeth put down her kickstand and collapsed next to Lois. "You did really well, Lois. Twenty-two miles at more than twenty-one dollars a mile. I'd need a pencil to figure it out, but that's a lot of money."

"I know. But I wonder how far Bruce Patman got?"

"Amy was following him. As soon as I get back home, I'll give her a call. Then I'll let you know."

Lois looked up at the sky. "He could have dropped out, I suppose."

"He probably did," Elizabeth said encouragingly. "You know how he loses interest in things."

"But he hasn't lost interest in showing me up," Lois said bitterly.

"Let's wait and see. You can never tell about Bruce Patman."

Fortunately, there were vans patrolling the route ready to take the riders and their bikes back to the Sweet Valley Middle School parking lot. There was no way Elizabeth could have ridden back by herself, and she knew Lois couldn't. Getting back home from the parking lot was effort enough.

At home she found Steven playing basketball in the driveway.

"Well, well, it's Elizabeth back from the Tour de France."

Elizabeth ignored Steven's sarcasm. "Where is everyone?"

"Mom and Dad went shopping. And Jessica hasn't come home yet. Don't tell me you stopped before she did?"

"Not exactly," Elizabeth said slowly.

Steven turned back to his game. "By the way, Amy called."

"Amy! Why didn't you tell me?" Elizabeth shrieked.

"I thought I just did," Steven muttered, but Elizabeth didn't hear him. She was already halfway to the kitchen. She grabbed the phone and dialed Amy's number.

After several rings, Amy finally answered.

"What took you so long?" Elizabeth demanded as soon as Amy said hello.

"It only rang four times," Amy said with a laugh.

"Sorry," Elizabeth said, "I'm just anxious to know what happened with Bruce."

"I'm afraid I can't tell you much," Amy said with a sigh.

"You can't? Why not?" Elizabeth asked.

"I followed him for eight miles," Amy said, "and then he just zoomed out of sight. That was the last I saw of him."

Elizabeth sat down on a kitchen chair. "So you don't know if he finished the whole bike-a-thon?"

"Not really. When I got to the finish line, I asked around but it was so crowded. No one remembered if Bruce had been there or not."

"That's too bad. I told Lois I'd call her to let her know how Bruce did," Elizabeth said.

"Patrick was at the finish line just like he was supposed to be. I asked him if he had seen Bruce, but he hadn't," Amy said. "But he did say that a lot of people came in around the same time and he hadn't gotten everyone's name for the *Sixers*."

"I guess we'll have to wait until Monday to find out," Elizabeth said.

"How did Lois do?" Amy asked.

"She went twenty-two miles," Elizabeth answered.

"That's great. But it's too bad she didn't finish," Amy said. "Then she would have beaten Bruce for sure."

Elizabeth agreed. "Lois's only chance is if Bruce didn't finish either. I think it's great you did the whole thing. It was a tough ride."

"I know. I'm in no hurry to do another one," said Amy.

"I know the feeling. My legs are really stiff," Elizabeth said.

"I guess I'll wait until tomorrow to get my ice cream sundae at Casey's."

"What sundae?" Elizabeth asked.

"That's right, you don't know. There was a special prize for everyone who went all thirty miles. We all got certificates for ice cream sundaes at Casey's Place," Amy said.

"Wow!" Elizabeth exclaimed.

"And you know how big they are. I don't think I could finish one by myself so . . ." she said temptingly.

"You'd share?"

"I sure would. Let's go tomorrow afternoon," Amy suggested.

"Thanks, Amy. That would be great," Elizabeth said.

After she hung up with Amy, Elizabeth called Lois to tell her all she knew about Bruce's progress. Then she went up to her room and took a nap for the rest of the afternoon. She didn't stir until the sound of water dripping in the bathroom woke her. Opening her eyes, Elizabeth realized that Jessica must not have turned one of the faucets all the way off.

With a sigh, she got out of bed, went into the bathroom, and turned off the water. Then she peeked into Jessica's bedroom. Her sister was lying on her bed, staring dreamily at the ceiling.

"You look like a person who's just heard the latest Johnny Buck album," Elizabeth commented.

"Oh, Lizzie," Jessica said, propping herself up on her elbows. "It was fabulous."

Elizabeth sat down on the edge of the bed. "Well, let's hear all about it."

That was all the invitation Jessica needed. She described every song, the album cover, the liner notes, the band, and the backup singers. Then, she lay back down on the bed. "Anyway, it was great," she finished.

"I can tell," Elizabeth said with a laugh. "Who else was at Lila's?"

"Everyone! Janet and Ellen and Scott Joslin, a couple of other Unicorns, and a few more seventh-grade boys. Bruce Patman showed up, too."

Elizabeth snapped to attention. "Bruce? What time did he get to Lila's?"

"I wasn't really paying attention," Jessica said.

"Think about it," Elizabeth urged. If Bruce had

gotten to Lila's early, he couldn't have finished the race.

"Elizabeth, I don't know. We were just listening to the music; I barely noticed the time."

"Do you remember when you got there?" Elizabeth asked.

"A little after one," Jessica admitted.

That was awfully early. "How far did you ride, Jess?"

"I'm not saying." Jessica giggled.

"Oh, yes you are," Elizabeth said, pouncing on her sister and tickling her.

"Stop it!" Jessica shrieked.

"I will when you tell me how far you rode," Elizabeth said.

"All right, all right. Four miles."

"Four miles? That's it?" Elizabeth stopped tickling Jessica and stood by the bed.

"Yes," Jessica replied. "The four-mile checkpoint was the closest to Lila's house, so I just stopped there."

Four miles! Elizabeth was shocked. "Did Bruce get there much after you?" she asked.

"Boy, Lizzie, you sure are interested in Bruce today." Jessica eyed her with curiosity.

"I'm trying to figure out if he beat Lois in the bike-a-thon. She went twenty-two miles."

"Well, he must have beaten Lois." Jessica wrinkled her nose. "But come to think of it, he did show up pretty soon after I did."

Elizabeth gasped. "I wonder if he really finished."

Jessica got up, went over to her mirror, and started fixing her hair. "He probably did. Don't forget he has that great bike."

"I guess," Elizabeth said, but she didn't sound convinced.

The next day, while she was waiting with Amy for a free sundae at Casey's, Elizabeth told her friend everything that Jessica had said. "I think that's pretty good news. Lois may stand a chance of winning," she finished.

"I think so, too," Amy replied. "Have you told Lois yet?"

"No. I didn't want to get her hopes up. We'll know more tomorrow at school."

"Well, I'm ready to write my article for the *Sixers* on how it feels to ride thirty miles." Amy stretched her legs out in front of her. "Terrible."

"Here comes something that should make you feel better, Amy," Elizabeth said, nodding her head in the direction of the waiter who was carrying a huge ice cream sundae. With a flourish, he put it down in front of them. "Girls, your super-duper bike-a-thon sundae special."

Mountains of vanilla and chocolate ice cream were piled into an oversized sundae glass. Rivers of hot fudge sauce were melting the ice cream, and whipped cream covered everything. One lone cherry sat on top.

"Wow," Amy said.

"I've never seen such a gigantic sundae!" Elizabeth exclaimed.

"Me either," Amy said. She took a spoonful of the ice cream and swallowed a huge bite. "I could go another thirty miles for another one of these."

After the girls had finished the entire sundae, Elizabeth headed home. When she arrived, she found Steven reading in his room and asked him for the $1.10 he owed her.

"Can I give it to you later?" Steven asked. "I don't get my allowance until tomorrow."

Elizabeth shook her head. "No way, Steven. I want to bring my pledges in tomorrow." She pointed to a large metal football-shaped bank on his desk. "You can take it out of there."

Steven grudgingly agreed. "I suppose I should

get Jessica's money out, too. How much will I owe her?"

Elizabeth laughed. "I think you can afford it. Twenty cents."

"That's it?" Steven asked with surprise.

"That's right," Elizabeth answered. "She only rode four miles."

"Do Mom and Dad know that?"

"No," Elizabeth said seriously. "And I don't think they're going to be very happy when they find out."

It didn't take long for the subject to come up. Later that evening, Mr. Wakefield stuck his head into Jessica's room, where the twins were studying, and said, "What do I owe you two for the bike-a-thon?"

Jessica blushed.

"You rode twenty-two miles, didn't you, Elizabeth?" Mr. Wakefield asked. "What about you, Jessica?"

"Uh, four miles," Jessica said in a low voice.

Mr. Wakefield wrinkled his brow. "I don't get it. What happened?"

"I just didn't feel like riding any more than that," Jessica said with a shrug.

"But you felt like going to Lila's house, I suppose. I've been hearing about that Johnny Buck album all day," Mr. Wakefield said sternly.

"I went there after I finished the bike-a-thon. You and Mom said I could go when I was done."

Mr. Wakefield shook his head. "Jessica, I'm disappointed in you. You knew that we meant you could go when you had ridden as far as you could."

"I'm sorry, Dad. It's just that my legs were getting *so* tired."

"Well, I guess I can say you've saved me some money," Mr. Wakefield said, pulling his wallet from his pocket. "But I'm not happy about it."

He handed Elizabeth her money, and then gave four dollars to Jessica. "I wish you had been a little more honest," he said before leaving the room.

Jessica could feel tears coming to her eyes. She hated to disappoint her father. Going to Lila's after riding only four miles had seemed like such a good idea at the time. And now it seemed like the worst idea in the world.

Eight

◇

The excitement over the bike-a-thon hadn't worn off over the weekend. The whole middle school was buzzing about it when the twins arrived at school on Monday.

Everyone was comparing experiences. Some were complaining about how tired they had felt on Saturday night. Jessica, not wanting to have it widely known that she had quit after only four miles, joined right in.

The other, more exciting topic was which rider had made the most money and won the mountain bike. A number of riders had finished the race, but for the most part, they didn't have many sponsors. Everyone was curious about how Lois had done. When Elizabeth told the group in the hallway that Lois had ridden twenty-two miles, everyone was impressed.

"That's pretty good," Grace Oliver commented. "I wonder how far Bruce rode."

"I think we're about to find out, because here he comes," Amy announced.

Bruce Patman strode to his locker. He was grinning from ear to ear. "You're looking at the winner of the mountain bike," he declared, looking around at the crowd. His gaze fell on Amy. "What happened to you? I thought you were supposed to be keeping up with me. I turned around and you were gone."

"I rode eight miles with you, Bruce," Amy said angrily. "The real question is, what happened to *you*?"

"Only eight? Then you missed the other twenty-two miles. I rode the whole way."

"You did?" Elizabeth asked in astonishment. How had he made it to Lila's so early?

Bruce glared at Elizabeth. "Don't you believe me?"

"I didn't say that!" Elizabeth answered.

"Well, maybe you'll believe this." Bruce whipped

a green piece of paper out of his pocket and shoved it toward Elizabeth. It was a check for six hundred dollars. Elizabeth had never held such a large check in her hand before. It made her a little nervous, so she handed it back to Bruce.

The others begged to have a look at it. They oohed and aahed as they passed it around.

"Hey, you guys, careful with that," Bruce ordered. "My parents didn't mind paying up, but they may not want to do it twice if one of you tears the check." He turned to Elizabeth. "Are you convinced now that I rode the whole way?"

"I guess so," she said unhappily.

"I suppose you'll be putting my picture on the front page of your newspaper," he went on. "With a nice big article, too."

"I'll see what I can do," Elizabeth muttered.

"You know, if Lois Waller had won, you would have splashed *her* picture all over the paper. And it would have taken up a lot more room than mine." He laughed at his own joke; a couple of others joined in.

"Come on, Elizabeth, let's get out of here," Amy said, pulling on her friend's arm.

"Don't be mad at me, girls. Think of all the

great video equipment this money is going to buy for the school," Bruce called after them.

"I suppose he's right," Amy said. "But I don't know if that will make Lois feel any better."

"Lois!" Elizabeth said. "Who's going to tell her? We can't let Bruce break the news to her."

"You're right. If he tells her, it will be awful! Bruce will really rub it in."

"I guess I should do it," Elizabeth said.

"Good idea. She'll probably take it best from you," Amy said reassuringly.

"Well, she told me she'd be in school by lunch-time, after her dentist appointment. I'll look for her in the cafeteria," Elizabeth said with a sigh.

At noon, Elizabeth glanced around the cafeteria, hoping to catch a glimpse of Lois, but she was nowhere in sight. Elizabeth sat down to eat her lunch with Grace Oliver and Cammi Adams. She was just about to bite into her chicken salad sandwich when she spotted Lois at the milk counter. She hurried over and tapped Lois on the shoulder. "Why don't you come over and sit with us?"

"Sure," Lois said. She peered at Elizabeth. "Bruce won, didn't he?"

Elizabeth nodded slowly. "I'm sorry, Lois."

Before Lois could answer, Bruce came sauntering up to them. "Hey, Walrus, did your pal give you the news?" he asked jovially.

"Yes," Lois answered quietly.

"Aren't you going to congratulate me?"

"I guess so."

"So say it. Say, 'Congratulations, Bruce. I went only twenty-two miles, and you finished the course.' "

"She doesn't have to say anything if she doesn't want to," Elizabeth said.

"I don't mind congratulating him for winning fair and square," Lois spoke up. Then she turned and walked over to the table where Cammi and Grace were waiting.

Bruce stood staring at Lois, not sure if he had won that round or not. With a scowl on his face, he turned away from Elizabeth. He was joined by Scott Joslin.

"Hey, buddy, you really gave it to old Lois." Scott punched Bruce on the shoulder.

Bruce's face cleared. "Yeah, I sure did."

"You ought to give her a consolation prize, considering you won the bike that she wanted so badly."

Bruce gave a short, harsh laugh. "What should I give her?"

"How about your gift certificate? We all know how much Lois likes to eat!"

"What?" Bruce asked, clearly confused. "You mean she would eat a gift certificate?"

Now it was Scott's turn to look confused. Then he started laughing. "Good one, Patman. I suppose if she was hungry enough, she *would* eat the gift certificate instead of the ice cream."

Bruce and Scott headed back to their table, but Elizabeth stood in front of the milk counter, thinking over the boys' conversation. There was something wrong with it. It took her a few seconds to figure out just what it was. Then she realized. Bruce had looked puzzled when Scott mentioned the gift certificate. He must have received one like everyone else who finished the race. Elizabeth couldn't stop wondering why Bruce didn't seem to know about it.

When Elizabeth was getting some books from her locker at the end of the school day, she spotted Lois down the hall. "Lois," she called, shutting her locker and hurrying over to her. "Would you like to come home with me after school?"

Lois hesitated. "I was going to go over to

the retirement home and start collecting my pledges."

"Why don't you wait until tomorrow? You've got all week to collect the money."

"That's true. Sure," Lois agreed.

Wanting to keep Lois's mind off Bruce Patman and the bike-a-thon, Elizabeth chattered the whole way home. But when they were walking up to the Wakefield house, Elizabeth said, "You know, I think the way you stood up to Bruce at lunchtime was great."

"I didn't do anything," Lois said.

"Yes, you did. You didn't get upset by his stupid teasing."

"I'm used to it by now." Lois's voice rose a little. "I wonder what Bruce is going to do with two bikes?"

"Probably get bored with both of them," Elizabeth said.

"I don't know how he always manages to come out on top," Lois said.

Elizabeth opened the door to her house. She was relieved that Jessica wasn't home. Elizabeth loved her twin more than anyone else in the world, but she knew she could be rude to people like Lois Waller, who weren't in her crowd.

Dropping her books on the kitchen table, Elizabeth said, "How about a snack?" She opened the refrigerator door and peered inside. "We could have ham sandwiches or turkey." Then she looked in the freezer compartment. "Or ice cream."

"I'm trying to stick to a diet," Lois said shyly.

Elizabeth turned and looked at her friend. "That's wonderful."

"I've lost two pounds already. I guess that bike-a-thon was good for something."

"Let's have some fruit then," Elizabeth said, bringing the fruit bowl from the kitchen counter over to the table.

"Thanks," Lois said, helping herself to a peach.

The girls were interrupted by the sound of the front door opening. Jessica came into the kitchen a second later.

"Hi, Jess," Elizabeth said.

"Hello." Jessica stared at Elizabeth with a look that said, what is Lois Waller doing in my house?

"Do you want any fruit?" Elizabeth asked.

"Fruit?" Jessica wrinkled her nose. "No thanks." She went to the freezer and helped herself to a heaping dish of chocolate-swirl ice cream. Then she joined her sister and Lois at the table.

She turned to Lois. "I hear things didn't go very well for you at the bike-a-thon."

"I wouldn't say that, exactly. I rode twenty-two miles."

"Jessica," Elizabeth said, breaking into the conversation. "Was Bruce excited when he showed up at Lila's on Saturday?"

"Excited? Why should he have been excited?"

"Well, he had just finished the race. He must have guessed he was going to win."

"He was dirty, and kind of cranky, but I guess I would be, too, if I had ridden that far."

"How far did you ride?" Lois asked sweetly.

Jessica looked embarrassed for a moment. Then she said, "I got a cramp in my leg, so I had to quit early." She hopped out of her chair. "I'm going to take my ice cream upstairs," she said. "See you later."

The second she was gone, Elizabeth said, "How did you know Jessica quit so soon, Lois?"

"I overheard her talking to Lila about it," Lois confessed. "Why were you so interested in Bruce and how he looked when he got to Lila's?"

Elizabeth hesitated. "When I've got it all figured out, I'll tell you."

Lois looked at her curiously, but all she said was, "Whenever you're ready."

"Let's go up to my room," Elizabeth said.

A little while later Mrs. Waller came to pick up Lois.

There was still a half hour before Elizabeth had to take the chili out of the freezer and put it in the microwave. She couldn't get Bruce Patman out of her mind, so she decided to go into the backyard to her thinking seat under the big pine tree. That was where the twins had always gone as little girls when they wanted to be alone. And even though Jessica thought it was too immature for them now, Elizabeth still liked to go there when she had a problem to work out. She thought if she organized her thoughts on paper, they might begin to make sense.

Grabbing a pad and pencil from a kitchen drawer, Elizabeth wandered outside, and settled into her usual spot.

On the top of the yellow pad, she wrote in big black letters, BRUCE PATMAN. Underneath she wrote BIKE-A-THON. She thought for a few minutes and then started to write.

1. Bruce said he rode the whole course, but

he got to Lila's just after Jessica. Did he have time to ride thirty miles?

2. Jessica said Bruce didn't look excited. He seemed cranky, which was a funny way to act if he had just won the bike-a-thon.

3. Bruce didn't seem to know about the gift certificate to Casey's that everyone got at the end of the course!

Elizabeth tapped her pencil on the pad for a moment. Then she wrote:

DID BRUCE PATMAN REALLY FINISH THE RACE?

Nine

◇

"Did you have a good time at Elizabeth's house?" Mrs. Waller asked Lois.

"Yes. She's really nice," Lois answered.

Mrs. Waller smiled at her daughter. "I'm glad you two are friends."

"Me, too," Lois agreed.

"I left some meat loaf for you in the refrigerator. You can warm it up in the microwave when you're ready for dinner. There's some fresh lemonade, too."

"Mom," Lois said hesitantly, "can I come to the retirement home with you?" She really didn't want to put it off until the next day.

"Now?"

"Yes. I'd like to start collecting my pledges. I was going to go right after school, but Elizabeth invited me over . . ."

"Of course, dear. I'll run you home during my break."

"It's not going to be easy to tell Mrs. Williams and the rest of them that I didn't win." Lois sighed.

"They'll be proud of you, Lois, I'm sure. I know *I* am."

Everybody at the retirement home was glad to see Lois when she came in.

Lois went over and took a seat on the couch next to Mr. Shand. "How are you?" she asked.

"I'm fine. But how are *you*? We've been waiting to hear about the big race. Haven't we, Lily?"

Mrs. Williams nodded. "We certainly have. Let me round up the rest of your sponsors." Mrs. Williams got out of her chair. Soon, a small group was gathered around Lois.

"So, Lois, tell us all about the bike-a-thon," a woman named Mrs. Klein said.

Lois looked down at her shoes. "First of all, I guess I have to tell you, I came in second." She glanced up, but no one seemed particularly upset by this news.

"Second place!" Mr. Shand nodded. "That's very good."

"I rode twenty-two miles."

"That's a long distance," one of the men said. "I couldn't even ride ten miles anymore."

Mr. Shand laughed. "I bet you couldn't do twenty-two miles when you were Lois's age, either."

The man laughed along with him. "Maybe not."

Mrs. Klein patted her hand. "Tell us the whole story."

Lois went into a detailed explanation of how the bike-a-thon worked, what the riders had gotten in their kits, and what the bike trail was like. She knew that some of the residents didn't get out much, so she tried to make her story as interesting as possible.

When she had finished, Mrs. Williams said, "Lois, you left out one important detail."

"I did?"

"Yes. Who won?"

"Oh." Lois had been trying to forget about Bruce. "It was a boy named Bruce Patman. He . . . he isn't very nice to me."

"Oh, yes," Mrs. Williams said. "You told me about Bruce the other day. Well, don't let him get to you. He'll get his comeuppance."

"I hope so," Lois replied, "but it hasn't happened yet."

The older people looked around at one another and nodded. Then Mrs. Klein said, "When you get to be as old as we are, Lois, you'll see that a lot of people eventually get what they deserve."

Lois shrugged. It might happen, but how could she be sure she would live to see it?

"Mom, can I ride over to Amy's house after we finish eating?"

The Wakefield family was sitting outside on their patio, enjoying barbecued hamburgers prepared by Mr. Wakefield.

"You won't stay long, will you?" Mrs. Wakefield said, looking at her watch. "I don't want you riding your bike back when it's dark."

"No, I won't. Especially if I can leave right away." Elizabeth glanced over at her sister. Technically, it was Elizabeth's turn to clear the table, but she had done Jessica's chores so many times, it only seemed fair for Jessica to do this one, small job.

Jessica made a face. "Mom, I told Lila I'd call right after dinner."

"That's really important," Steven commented through a mouthful of hamburger. "The world might collapse if you don't call Lila immediately after you eat."

"I think you could help your sister out, Jessica," Mr. Wakefield said. "After all, she helps you a lot with your chores."

"But she wants to help me," Jessica protested. She turned to her sister. "Tell them, Liz."

"Sometimes I do, and sometimes I don't," Elizabeth said firmly.

"Well, it's not like I twist your arm or anything," Jessica said huffily.

"That's enough, girls," Mrs. Wakefield said. "Elizabeth, you can go to Amy's now, and Jessica will clear the table. Tomorrow night when it's Jessica's turn, you can help her."

Elizabeth rode her bike to Amy's house. When she arrived, she found Amy poring over the layout of the latest issue of *The Sweet Valley Sixers*. The pages were spread out on the Suttons' living room floor.

Together they began deciding where the different articles should be placed. Then they read each one over to make sure there were no misspellings or grammatical mistakes.

After a while Amy got up to stretch. "We don't have a picture of Bruce, you know," she commented.

"I know. But I don't care. Besides . . ."

"Besides what?" Amy asked, flopping back down on the floor.

"Amy, this may sound crazy, but I'm not sure Bruce won the race at all."

Amy's eyes grew wide. "You're kidding!"

"No, I'm not," Elizabeth said. She told Amy her reasons for thinking Bruce had not finished the bike-a-thon.

When she had finished explaining, Amy cried, "It all makes sense! I couldn't believe it when I lost Bruce after eight miles. Sure, he was going fast, but I kept thinking somewhere along the way I would catch up to him. I never did. He just dropped out of sight!"

"Really? That's all the more reason to think my suspicions are right."

"And if Bruce lost, that means Lois won!" Amy said. Her eyes shone.

"Wouldn't that be great? She could get the mountain bike, and everyone would make a big fuss over her. Lois could use some attention like that."

"There's just one thing, Elizabeth. How can we prove that Bruce didn't finish the race?"

"Good question. Do you have any ideas?"

"No. After all, his parents gave him a check for six hundred dollars. He must have showed them a punched card."

Elizabeth got off the floor and wiped a few bits of paper from her jeans. "You're right, Amy. Proving Bruce didn't win the race wouldn't be easy."

"It might be impossible," Amy added.

Elizabeth hoped not, but she knew that what Amy said was true. "I've got to get going."

"What about the paper?" Amy asked.

"I don't think we should turn it in yet. Not if there's a chance that Bruce didn't *earn* his money fair and square."

Amy nodded, then said goodbye. Elizabeth hopped on her bike and rode through the park.

A baseball game was breaking up, and she noticed several of the seventh- and eighth-grade boys going off in different directions. When Elizabeth pedaled a little more quickly to see who was there, she noticed Bruce Patman. She stopped when he called out her name. "When's your newspaper coming out?" Bruce demanded. "I can't wait to see the story about me."

"It won't be out for a couple of days."

Elizabeth was ready to pedal off when she realized that Bruce was not riding his bike. Everybody knew he rode it everywhere since the day he got it. It seemed very strange to see him walking.

"How come you're walking tonight?" she asked.

Bruce scowled. "What do you mean?"

"I mean where's your fancy bike?"

"I'm sick of it. Maybe I rode too much in that bike-a-thon."

Elizabeth didn't believe him, but she only remarked, "Then I guess it's a good thing you rode all thirty miles."

Bruce looked blank. "Huh?"

"Because you've won the mountain bike," Elizabeth prompted. "Since you're sick of your racer, you can ride the mountain bike instead. Bye, Bruce," she yelled as she rode off.

The mystery seemed even deeper now. Elizabeth was sure something must have happened to

Bruce's bike, or he would have been riding it. Now, if she could only find out what!

After putting her own bike away, Elizabeth burst into the house. She was eager to find her pad of paper to add the latest bit of information she had about Bruce.

Elizabeth looked in her room, in the kitchen and in the den, but the pad was nowhere to be seen. When she went back upstairs to check her room again, she happened to glance into Jessica's room.

Jessica was sitting cross-legged on her bed. The pad of paper was in her hand.

"Jess, where did you find that?" Elizabeth grabbed the pad from her sister.

"It was on your desk. I needed a pencil, and when I went to get one, I saw this."

"Well, you didn't have to read it!"

"You're always against Bruce," Jessica burst out. "Why?"

"I don't like the way he treats people. Anyway, now that you've read this, you can see that something doesn't add up about Bruce and the bike-a-thon."

Jessica swung her feet off the bed. "I don't see that at all! Bruce won. You forget he didn't even have to enter that silly bike-a-thon, since he didn't need the prize."

"For your information, I just saw him a few minutes ago. He was walking, not riding."

"So, what does that prove? Maybe he just felt like walking."

"I don't think so," Elizabeth said.

"So, are you saying that Bruce couldn't have beaten Lois?"

"No," Elizabeth admitted. "I'm sure he could, but I'm still convinced he cheated. I just haven't figured out how."

"And you won't," Jessica replied. "Bruce had no reason to cheat."

Elizabeth turned and started walking to her own room. "I guess we'll just have to wait and see whether Bruce won or not."

Jessica followed her. "You wouldn't want to make a bet on that, would you?"

"What do you mean?"

"I'll bet you that Bruce really did win the race."

"I don't want to bet, Jessica," Elizabeth said.

"Then you know you can't prove it," Jessica said with satisfaction.

"I told you, we'll have to wait and see."

"Look, not accepting the bet is the same as

admitting you're wrong. It's a matter of princi-
ple," Jessica said righteously.

Elizabeth turned and faced her twin. "All right,
let's bet then. What's the prize?"

"Whoever wins has to do the other one's chores
for a week. I didn't really enjoy cleaning up the
kitchen for you tonight, you know," she added.

Elizabeth didn't mention how often she had
filled in for Jessica.

"So, is it a bet?" Jessica demanded.

"I guess so."

"Let's shake on it," Jessica said, putting out
her hand.

Elizabeth took it reluctantly. "It's a bet."

Ten

◇

Elizabeth was not in her usual cheerful mood as she dressed for school the next morning. She put on a blue checked shirt and a denim skirt, barely noticing how she looked. The more she thought about it, the less likely it seemed that she could actually prove her suspicions about Bruce.

Jessica, on the other hand, was in a wonderful mood. Elizabeth could hear her humming a Johnny Buck tune as she took her shower. When she'd finished, Jessica popped her head into Elizabeth's room.

"You know, Lizzie, I've been thinking. We ought to set a time limit on our bet."

"A time limit! Proving Bruce cheated is going to be hard enough without a time limit."

"You can't go on trying to prove it forever. All the money is due by Friday, and then Bruce will be declared the official winner. Why don't we say you have until Friday to show everyone that Bruce cheated?"

"But that's only three days away," Elizabeth objected. Then, before Jessica could answer, she said, "Oh, what's the difference? Friday's all right, I guess." If she couldn't prove anything by Friday, she probably could never do it.

"Good." Jessica's tone was smug. "Then you can do my chores, starting on Saturday."

Elizabeth groaned. Saturday was the day the twins stripped their sheets and remade the beds, a job they both hated.

When Elizabeth got to school, she pulled Amy aside before they went into homeroom and told her everything that had happened since she last saw her, from seeing Bruce without his bike to making her bet with Jessica.

"Wow!" Amy said. "You've been busy. There really are a lot of coincidences that don't add up to Bruce Patman winning that bike."

"But I have to prove it. We can't just print

suspicions in the newspaper. Jessica doesn't believe me, and others probably wouldn't, either."

"Well, let's find some proof, then. What about Bruce's bike?" Amy asked.

"His bike? I told you, he wasn't riding it."

"So maybe it's broken," Amy said. "If it is, he couldn't have finished the bike-a-thon."

"How would we find out something like that?"

"Easy. We'll look in his garage," Amy said.

"You mean sneak over to the Patmans'?"

"Bruce usually stays after school to play soccer on Tuesdays," Amy reminded Elizabeth.

"Even if his bike is banged up, it doesn't really prove anything. He could always say that it broke after the bike-a-thon," Elizabeth said.

"I guess you're right," Amy agreed.

"There's got to be some way to show that Bruce cheated," Elizabeth said. "But I don't know what it is."

"Why don't we start by asking people if they saw Bruce finish?"

"That's a good idea," Elizabeth said. "If Bruce was at the finish line, at least one or two other people would have seen him. We've got a list of everyone who finished to put in the *Sixers*."

"Let's divide up the list and start asking kids if they saw Bruce," Amy suggested.

"Well, we can't be too obvious, or everyone will start wondering why we're asking," Elizabeth said.

"That's true," Amy agreed. "But we can ask the kids we know well."

"All right, I'll start with Ken Matthews and Grace Oliver."

Elizabeth found Ken in the hallway between classes.

"Ken," she said hesitantly, "can I talk to you for a second?"

"Sure, what's up?"

"You finished the bike-a-thon, right?" Elizabeth asked.

"Yes. Now I'm sorry I didn't collect more pledges. I could have won that mountain bike instead of Bruce. He sure doesn't need one."

Elizabeth was happy that Ken had given her an easy opening. "By the way," she said, "did you see him on the course when you were riding?"

"No, come to think of it, I didn't. Of course I wasn't exactly looking for him," Ken said.

"Did you see him at the finish line?" Elizabeth asked.

Ken thought about it for a few moments. "No, not then either. And I hung around for a while after I got punched in. Why are you asking?"

"I was just wondering," was all Elizabeth said.

At lunch Elizabeth and Amy compared notes. "No one I talked to saw Bruce," Amy reported.

"Same here. But does that really say he wasn't there?" Elizabeth asked.

"Well, it's certainly something to add to your list," Amy said, biting into her sandwich.

"But it's still not final proof." Elizabeth sighed.

"I'm afraid the kind of proof we're looking for only comes when the suspect confesses."

Elizabeth stared at Amy. "A confession! That's it! That's exactly what we need."

"Come on, Elizabeth, you don't think Bruce Patman would actually confess to cheating, do you?"

"No, not if he knew he was confessing . . ." Elizabeth's voice trailed off.

"Elizabeth, what are you planning?"

"I'm not sure yet. But I do know one thing. The only person who can tell us exactly what happened is Bruce Patman himself."

Jessica was lying in a lounge chair on the Wake-

fields' patio, listening to a tape of "Pass the Buck."
She was also thinking about Elizabeth trying to
prove Bruce didn't ride all thirty miles of the
bike-a-thon. Elizabeth had looked pretty grim.
And she had good reason. She was going to lose
that bet for sure. Jessica smiled at the thought. A
whole week of no chores—now, that was something to look forward to.

There was one thought that nagged at Jessica,
though. As she thought back to the afternoon of
the bike-a-thon, it did seem that Bruce had gotten to Lila's house awfully early to have finished
the whole course.

She, Ellen, Janet, and Lila had been sitting
around listening to "Pass the Buck." Scott Joslin,
Charlie Cashman, and Jerry McAllister were there,
too.

Jessica remembered the first song, "Bad Ap-
ples," a fast number, that she had wanted to get
up and dance to. The next song was slow and
romantic. The boys had pretended to gag. Right
after that song, Bruce had come in.

Jessica remembered it very clearly. Bruce had
looked disheveled and angry.

"Hey, what's wrong?" Charlie had asked.

"Nothing," Bruce had snapped.

"Is the bike-a-thon over already?" Lila had asked.

"It is for me."

"Did you finish?" Lila had asked.

Bruce had hesitated. "Of course I did," he finally said.

"You must have ridden awfully fast," Scott had commented.

"That's right. With a bike like mine, I made it in record time!" Bruce had boasted.

There had been no more discussion of the bike-a-thon, but now Jessica wondered if it was possible that Bruce had not finished after all. She pushed the nagging thought out of her mind. If Bruce hadn't finished, she would lose her bet, and she would get stuck with Elizabeth's chores for a week! She certainly did not want that to happen.

Jessica opened her eyes and saw Elizabeth standing over her. "Hi, Lizzie," she said. "Coming out to catch some rays?"

"No, I'm working on something." She held up her pad with the information about Bruce.

"I thought you were about ready to give up."

"No way." Elizabeth smiled. "I've just got to figure out the details of my plan."

"What plan?"

"You'll see," was all Elizabeth would say.

Jessica didn't like the sound of that. But before she could question her sister further, Elizabeth headed over to her thinking spot.

Once again, Elizabeth went over the facts in what she was beginning to think of as the Bruce Patman case. The facts added up, and now Elizabeth had an idea about how to make Bruce admit he cheated. It was going to take some luck, but Elizabeth was counting on Bruce's enormous ego to make it work. She also needed the cooperation of one other person. Elizabeth got up and went into the house. She was glad to see that Jessica was still outside sunning herself. Elizabeth would need some privacy when she talked to Lois.

"Your time is running out. Deadline's tomorrow, you know," Jessica reminded Elizabeth on Thursday morning.

"I know. Be sure to be in the cafeteria at lunchtime today," Elizabeth said.

"Where else would I be?" Jessica said with a laugh.

"I don't know, but just be there," Elizabeth answered.

In truth, Elizabeth had been worried about how to get things off the ground. She needed to start a conversation with Bruce, but she had not thought of a good way to do it.

Fortunately, Bruce took care of that himself. Lois, Elizabeth, and Amy were sitting at their table, discussing the best way to approach Bruce, when he walked up to them, a smirk on his face.

"Well, Lois. Have you handed in your money for the bike-a-thon yet?"

"Yes, I have," Lois answered quietly.

"How did it feel to know that you had spent all that time collecting pledges, and still lost? Kind of a waste of time, wasn't it, Lois?"

"It was hardly a waste of time," Amy cut in. "The purpose of the bike-a-thon was to raise money for our school library, and Lois did a good job of that."

"Not as good as I did," Bruce boasted.

"Oh, Bruce, give it up," said Amy.

Lois pushed her glasses up. "That's all right, Amy. Bruce has a point."

"I do?"

"Sure you do. Thinking that I could beat you was really dumb," Lois said.

Bruce eyed her suspiciously. "You mean you finally realize that?"

"I'd have to be pretty silly not to," Lois answered.

"I guess you would," Bruce said, starting to smile.

As Elizabeth had hoped, people were beginning to notice that Bruce and Lois were deep into a conversation. The Unicorns, sitting off in a corner by themselves, were looking at Bruce, and several of the others were getting up to see what was going on.

Lois continued. "In fact, Bruce, I really wish I could be more like you."

"That would be kind of hard, wouldn't it, Lois?" Bruce said condescendingly.

"It certainly would," Lila Fowler said loudly. She and a few other Unicorns had joined the group that was now gathered around the lunch table.

Lois shrugged. "I suppose. But I guess if I had to lose the bike-a-thon, at least I lost to a real winner."

"Thirty miles is a long way to ride," Elizabeth added. "How long did it take you, Bruce?"

"We really should put that information in the *Sixers* article," Amy added.

Bruce shrugged. "Pretty long," he said.

Ken Matthews, who was standing nearby, said, "It took me a good two and a half hours."

"Yeah, it was about that," Bruce said uncomfortably.

Elizabeth and Lois exchanged quick glances. "So that means you finished at about two-thirty," Lois said.

"Well," Bruce muttered, "I do have a racing bike, not like the clunker Matthews was riding."

"Hey," Ken piped up, "my bike is a ten-speed, too. Nobody could have finished that course in less than two and a half hours. Not even you, Patman."

"Then what I don't understand," Lois said, "is how you could have gotten to Lila's house before two o'clock. You not only had to finish the bike-a-thon, you had to ride all the way over there. It doesn't seem possible."

"I, uh . . ." Bruce floundered.

Jessica and Lila looked at each other. Jessica wanted to say something in Bruce's defense, but nothing came to mind, at least nothing that would not be a lie.

"Don't worry," Lois said, finally breaking the uncomfortable silence. "I understand. You were so afraid that I would beat you, you had to cheat."

"Are you crazy?" Bruce cried. "Me afraid that you would beat me? There's no way you would have won if I hadn't crashed and smashed my bike after eight miles!"

Lois gave Bruce a broad smile. "Thank you, Bruce, that's just what we wanted to know."

"Yes, Bruce, thanks," Elizabeth added. "I guess I have a new headline for the next *Sixers*: LOIS WALLER WINS BIKE-A-THON!" And with that, she headed for the newspaper office.

The plan had worked more perfectly than she had imagined.

Eleven

◇

"It's here!" Elizabeth called, hurrying down the hallway, with several copies of the newspaper in her hand.

Lois was waiting outside the lunchroom for her. As soon as Elizabeth got close enough, Lois pulled the top issue out of her hand. Lois's picture was on the front page below the headline WALLER WINS.

"Come on, let's go sit down," Lois said. "I want to read every word."

Elizabeth watched Lois's excitement grow as she read the article.

"Oh, what a great quote from Bruce," Lois

said. She cleared her throat and read, " 'It was perfectly understandable that I would have a terrible accident,' Patman said, 'considering how incredibly fast I was going.' "

"Everyone in school knows the truth now," Elizabeth said.

"Imagine, he actually punched out the numbers himself before showing his mileage card to his parents!" Lois exclaimed.

"It's hard to believe, isn't it?" Elizabeth agreed.

"I wonder what his parents are going to do about the six hundred dollars. Will the school have to give it back?"

"That's a good question," Elizabeth said. "I haven't heard what the Patmans intend to do. It would be too bad if they took the money away from the library."

"Maybe we'll find out at the assembly this afternoon," Lois said.

To Lois's surprise, when it was time for the assembly to begin, she was a lot less nervous than she expected. It did feel strange to be sitting on the stage with Mr. Clark, the principal, and Ms. Luster, the librarian, but she quickly got used to it.

Since she was going to be the center of attention, Lois had taken care to dress nicely. She and her mother had gone shopping, and because she had lost a few more pounds, she was able to fit into a pretty blue dress. She'd had her hair trimmed, and it fell in soft waves around her face.

Ms. Luster spoke first. She thanked everyone for participating, and spoke a little about the video equipment and tapes they would soon be enjoying. Then Mr. Clark took the microphone.

"First of all, let me report to you that Sweet Valley Middle School can be very proud. You've raised over three thousand dollars for your library."

The assembled students broke out into cheers.

Then Mr. Clark turned somber. "Many of you know that there was some irregularity in the bike-a-thon. One student did not earn the amount he said he did. However, his parents have graciously agreed to let the school keep the money."

I hope his parents make him repay the six hundred dollars! Lois thought. How would Bruce ever manage that? When she thought of all the heartache Bruce had caused her, she couldn't feel very sorry for him. Whatever punishment his parents gave him, he deserved it.

"Now let us turn to a happier subject," Mr.

Clark continued. "We have on the stage a girl who worked very hard to earn over four hundred dollars for our school. Members of the PTA, guests, and boys and girls, let me introduce to you, Lois Waller."

There was thunderous applause as Lois walked up to the microphone. She looked out at the audience. Her mother, sitting in the front row, beamed proudly. Elizabeth, sitting near the front of the auditorium next to Amy, gave her the thumbs-up sign.

Lois cleared her throat. "It's a real honor to be standing up here. Getting the pledges was hard, but riding that twenty-two miles was harder."

Everyone laughed good-naturedly.

"I'm glad I was able to help my school and . . . well, that's it, I guess. Thank you."

The applause started again. Some people whistled and stamped their feet as Mr. Davis rolled out the bright-blue mountain bike.

Lois took the bike from Mr. Davis and stood with it as a photographer from the *Sweet Valley News* took her picture. This was one of the happiest moments of her life.

Elizabeth sat out on the patio and watched Jessica set the picnic table.

"Jess, I think Mom wants you to use the cloth napkins."

Jessica turned to her with a sigh. "Now you tell me? I just finished putting out the paper ones."

"Sorry, I didn't notice." She held up her book. "I was reading."

"And I still have to make the fruit salad. That would have been your job."

"*Would* have been." Elizabeth smiled mischievously. "It sure is nice having a week off."

"Elizabeth, if I ever offer to make a bet with you again, please don't take me up on it."

"I don't know about that." Elizabeth laughed. "Watching you work is the most fun I've had in a long time."

A short time later, the Wakefields were sitting around the picnic table, eating dinner.

"You know, Jessica," Mrs. Wakefield said with a smile, "normally, people remove the stems from strawberries before serving them."

"And I believe," Mr. Wakefield added, "that it is traditional to peel the bananas as well."

Elizabeth couldn't help it. She started to giggle.

"Don't complain," Steven said. "At least you

got a fork to eat with. Someone must have thought I didn't need one."

By this time, everyone was laughing—everyone except Jessica. She ate for a moment in silence.

"I had an awful lot of work to do around here tonight," she said finally, in a defensive tone. "You can't blame me if I messed up a few things!"

"Well, the chicken's fine," Elizabeth said. "But, of course, Mom made that."

Jessica gave Elizabeth an angry look, which only made Elizabeth giggle more.

"Mom," Steven asked, "do you think you could teach Jessica how to cook before you go away next week? I'm afraid I may starve!" Mrs. Wakefield had just announced that she was going to San Francisco on business the following week.

"I'm not going to be doing all of the cooking!" Jessica protested.

"No," Mrs. Wakefield said seriously. "But I'm counting on all of you kids to be responsible next week, and to help your father out as much as possible."

"I'm always responsible!" Jessica cried indignantly.

"Except when you're getting a D on your history test," Mr. Wakefield reminded her.

"Or forgetting to mail the bills I asked you to," Mrs. Wakefield put in.

"Not to mention forgetting my fork!" Steven added.

Jessica threw her napkin at Steven. "OK, OK," she said. "I get the message. But just wait! I'm going to be Miss Responsibility next week. You'll probably have to give me a medal for good conduct when you get home, Mom."

Will Jessica keep her promise? Find out in Sweet Valley Twins #39, JESSICA AND THE MONEY MIX-UP.